I0600819

MR. AUGUST

Calendar Boys Series

NICOLE S. GOODIN

Mr. August
Published by Nicole S. Goodin
ISBN: 978-0-9951206-5-5
Copyright 2019 by Nicole S. Goodin
All rights reserved. ©
First published August 2019

Cover design by Nicole Goodin
Images purchased from Shutterstock
Editing by Spell Bound

This book is a work of fiction. All names, characters, places and incidents either are products of the author's imagination or are used fictitiously. Any resemblance to events, places, or persons, living or dead, is purely coincidental.
The author acknowledges all song titles, song lyrics, film titles, film characters, trademarked statuses and brands mentioned in this book are the property of, and belong to, their respective owners.
Nicole S. Goodin is in no way affiliated with any of the brands, songs, musicians or artists mentioned in this book.

For all the babes born in August

CHAPTER ONE

Liam

I tug my collar a little higher as I step out of my apartment building and into the chilly morning air.

I forgot how freezing it gets around here in the wintertime.

I shrug my bag up onto my shoulder and set off towards the campus.

I know I'm prepared, but I still don't feel it. I've been moping around at home for six months now, and it feels like an eternity.

I go over a few of the lesson plans and class content I've been given from last year in my head and try to remember what I'm meant to do when I get there.

I know one thing; I'm not going to be doing jack shit without getting a coffee into me first.

I shiver as I cross the road and head towards the little coffee shop just around the corner. It still serves the best in town – that much hasn't changed while I've been gone at least.

I jog the last half a block in a futile attempt to warm up.

I torture myself with memories of warm sunny beaches as I pull the door open.

The warmth and sweet aroma of coffee fills my nostrils, and I inhale deeply as I step inside.

I line up and glance around the shop.

It's still fairly early, but there's bound to be at least a few students from the uni milling around, there always is.

I notice a big, burly-looking guy frowning at something on the screen of his laptop – he's bound to be here on some type of sports scholarship, then there's a group of three girls all giggling and sipping on huge cups of some elaborate drink, and another two guys that give me the distinct impression they spend more time smoking weed than they do studying.

I'm just about to turn around and face the counter again when she catches my eye.

A young brunette woman, her dark wavy hair falling around her shoulders and her pretty face etched in concentration as she clicks away on her mouse and studies something on the screen of her laptop.

I swallow the lump in my throat as I watch her. I can't seem to look away. She tips her head to the side; her lips turn up into a slight smile before she straightens again.

She's *beautiful*.

I don't know if she's a student or not, if I had to guess, I'd say not – she looks wise, somehow.

As though she can feel my eyes on her, her gaze drifts from the screen and meets mine.

I'm too absorbed in her to even consider the fact that I should look away, so I don't, I just stare, my heart beating rapidly against my rib cage.

She holds eye contact for a few seconds before dropping her head in embarrassment, her cheeks colouring with a pink blush.

Shit. I don't know what I'm doing. I'm *staring*.

A woman hasn't captured my attention like this in a long while, and I don't know how to deal with it.

I pull my eyes from her, and step forward in the line.

I order my flat white and wait to the side, intentionally keeping my eyes from wandering back in her direction.

No one likes a creepy staring dude.

"Liam." The guy making the drinks calls my name, and I take the takeaway cup from him gratefully.

I'd love to have the balls to go over and ask the pretty girl if I could join her, but that's not going to happen, so instead, I go back through the door I came in, and only once I'm back out in the cold do I glance back.

She's watching me leave, an intrigued expression on her face, and I can't help but give her a small grin. She returns it with a small, shy smile, and I feel like fist pumping the air.

I don't know what the hell that was, but that pull was insane.

I feel stupidly elated for the rest of the walk to campus. Even when I enter the photography studio and pull out my camera, I'm still smiling like an idiot.

I can't figure out what's come over me.

I sit my bag on a chair and get out my laptop and the textbook that I'll need for my first class.

I glance at my watch.

I've only got ten minutes until it starts.

I power up my laptop and make a few quick adjustments to a photo I've been editing while I wait for other people to start arriving.

Finally, I hear chatter in the hallway, and I grab a pen from my bag in preparation.

Students start filing in and I smile at a few of them. I'll be spending the rest of the year with them, ideally, I'd like to make a good first impression.

A few of the girls start whispering behind their hands to one another and giggling. I frown at them.

A couple of the guys give me a chin lift or a nod as they come in.

I turn my back on the class and scrawl my name across the white board, 'Mr. Conrad', as I hear the room fill up.

I turn back around and my eyes land directly on the young woman sitting at a bench right in the front row.

She gasps as she recognises me, and it takes every ounce of my self-control not to openly stare at her again like I did less than half an hour ago.

It's her.

The girl from the coffee shop.

Of course, she's my student.

CHAPTER TWO

Perry

I wipe my sweaty palms on my jeans and try my hardest to settle my racing pulse.

He's the reason all the girls were fixing their hair and make-up in the bathroom before class – he's the reason everyone has been whispering about the hot new teacher.

He *is* the hot new teacher.

And *damn*, the rumours weren't wrong.

He's unbelievably sexy.

I've never had a teacher that looks like this before, and right now I'm grateful for that.

I haven't got a clue how I'm meant to focus on this class with *him* here – the gorgeous man I caught staring at me at the café earlier. It's beyond distracting.

I was hoping I'd share a class with him after I watched him walk off in the direction of the campus, but this wasn't exactly what I had in mind.

"Is he even old enough to be our teacher?" I hiss to Maddy as she sits next to me, openly ogling Mr. Conrad.

"No idea," she whispers back, "but whoever thought it was a good idea to put that hotty in rooms full of hormone-driven teenagers, clearly needs their head read."

I try to muffle my giggle. She's not wrong about that.

I can't speak for anyone else in the room, but I'm sure I'm going to be a hell of a lot more distracted in this class than any of my others.

It's a shame too, photography was my favourite elective from my entire class schedule last year. It's my passion – what I want to do with my life, and now I'm probably going to fail, and all because a man makes butterflies erupt in my stomach.

"Welcome to photography, year three, semester two," he tells us and *Jesus*, even his voice is hot. "I'm Mr. Conrad, and I'll be your lecturer for the rest of this year. I have a bachelor of fine arts, majoring in photography, and I've spent about four years of my life as a photographer travelling around the globe and, more recently, working in advertising and personal photography."

I try to figure out how old that might make him, but I've never been good with numbers.

"P." Maddy nudges my knee under the table, and I scowl at her as I try and fail to calculate in my head.

"What?" I demand.

"Professor hotty wants us to write our names on that." She jabs her finger at the clipboard that the guy across the aisle is holding out for me.

I smile apologetically and take it from him.

I write my name on the square that represents the desk I'm sitting at.

Guess it's mine for the semester.

I seriously regret picking the front row now.

Even though this class is bound to have a lot of independent work, I doubt I'm going to be able to keep my distance from my sexy new teacher.

I slide the board to Maddy, and she adds her name before passing it back to the row behind us.

Mr. Conrad tells us to get out our laptops and bring up our favourite collections of our work from our studies so far.

I watch his mouth move, but I'm too scared to look higher to his eyes, in case I find them looking back at me.

Not that they will be.

I must have been mistaken this morning.

He's a university lecturer for crying out loud – the last thing he's going to be doing is checking out twenty-year-old students.

I need to get my head together and stop being such a girl.

I tug my computer out of my bag, set it on the table and wait for it to load up.

I frown again at the image I was working on all morning. I just can't seem to get it right.

I minimise it down and search through my folders for a series of photos I took last year – the ones that stand out to me the most.

Maddy is the model in these ones, her and her boyfriend Trevor, and a dark starry night's sky.

I spent many a sleepless night working on this piece for my final year two portfolio, but it was worth every minute of it with the marks I got back over the holidays.

I killed year two, and the first half of this year too, I just have to hope that the rest of year three goes even half as well for me.

"Alright, I'm going to be coming around to see your work throughout the class, so have it ready, but for now, if you could go onto the online forum and read through the course content for this semester, it outlines what is required from you for the duration of the course, what you'll be graded on and when."

I nod and pull up the information he's requested we read.

So far so good.

"Excuse me, sir," I hear Maddy's voice from next to me, and I cringe.

If I know Maddy – which I do – this is bound to be embarrassing.

"Yes, Miss..." he glances at the clipboard that has made its way back to the front and into his hands, "Miss Dean, what can I do for you?"

Maddy pops her gum and smirks at him. "Call me Maddy, and I was just wondering if you're new to the uni? I haven't seen you around before."

I can feel myself blushing, and I don't even know why – Maddy is the one looking at our new teacher like she wants to eat him alive, not *me*, but I still feel totally embarrassed.

I can still picture that sexy smile on his lips this morning, whether or not it was intended for me is irrelevant at this point – it still makes me feel like a teenager with a crush.

I guess technically I'm only a year over being exactly that.

"Yes, *Miss Dean*." He makes a point of ignoring her request for a first-name basis, and I can't help but grin. "I *am* new here, this is my first day, and you are my first class for the semester. I'm covering Mrs Bennett while she goes on maternity leave."

Well, what a way to start.

"I'm sure we'll all make you feel *more* than welcome." Maddy grins suggestively, and I just want the floor to swallow me whole.

"I hope so," he says, his voice amused, and when I risk a glance up, his eyes meet mine for the briefest of seconds.

He turns away, and I release a breath I didn't know I'd been holding.

"*Girl*, you're blushing," Maddy teases as Mr. Conrad passes by our desk, heading for the desk furthest from ours.

"Whatever."

"You *are*, I don't even blame you, P, they don't call him professor hotty for nothing."

I cover my face with my hands to hide my blush. "*No one* calls him that, Maddy. You just made it up right now."

"But they will." She smirks as she finally decides to get her own laptop out. Truthfully, I've got no idea how she's made it to year three with her laid-back attitude.

She's even less likely to pass with a distraction like Mr. Conrad in the class.

Maddy is crazy in love with Trevor, but they've always been big believers in the 'look but don't touch' rule in their relationship.

I peek at our new teacher over my shoulder. He's talking to the gangly-looking dude with the awful body odour who always sits at the back of every class.

My palms start to sweat again at the idea of having to speak to him directly about my photographs. I'm struggling to be in the same room as him, without actually having to form coherent sentences.

I try my best to read through the course outline, but I fail.

I've read the same paragraph about half a dozen times and I still have no idea what it says, all I can concentrate on is the sound of him coming closer and closer as he works his way through every student in the room.

I can hear him talking to Brooke, which means there's only one workstation left between him and me.

The thought of him coming close makes goosebumps break out on my skin.

"I don't know what to show him," Maddy grumbles as she flicks from folder to folder on her screen. "I hate them all equally."

I giggle. "What about the ones you did with the flowers?"

She scrunches up her nose in distaste. "Not those... Do you think he'd be opposed to seeing my collection of selfies instead? They really are my best work."

I shake my head in amusement. "I'm not sure that's what he had in mind."

"Nudes?" she asks hopefully, a smart-ass grin on her lips.

"Oh yeah, you should go for it, we'll find out if he's a tits or ass man," I drawl.

"Miss Jenkins." The smooth voice comes from behind me and my eyes widen.

Shit.

I turn slowly in my seat, all the while hoping that he didn't hear the remark that I just made.

That would *not* be a great first impression. Well, technically, *second* impression.

"Hi," I squeak.

His eyes roam over my face before settling on my eyes. He's got brilliant blue eyes that feel like they're seeing entirely too much when they look into mine.

My hand twitches in the direction of my bag, and I have to fight the urge I have to pull out my camera and photograph him – something I'm certain he wouldn't appreciate.

The corner of his mouth lifts – in amusement I assume, and I realise my jaw has fallen lax as I stare at him with my greedy eyes.

I snap it shut and give myself a mental pep talk about being considerably less pathetic for the rest of the semester.

His eyes drift from my face to the screen of my laptop.

"What have you got to show me, Miss Jenkins?"

I open my mouth and hope like hell that nothing about tits and asses comes out this time.

"This is my final collection from last year," I say as I stare at my screen.

Maybe if I don't look at him, it won't be so hard to focus on making sense.

He leans further across my desk, so he can see better, and sweet baby Jesus, now I can smell him.

This is not good.

"May I?" he asks as he points to the mouse pad.

I nod my head.

He shifts the laptop slightly in his direction and reaches for the mouse pad, his arm brushing mine as he does.

I pull it away like he's scolded me, the zing of electricity left in its wake tingling like crazy.

I feel his eyes on my face again, but I don't look across at him.

He's too close. I don't feel in control at all.

He clicks on the mouse, once, twice, and then over, and over, and over again until he's viewed each image about half a dozen times.

"These are really good," he says, his voice soft, and perhaps a little surprised.

"Thank you," I mumble shyly.

I know they're good, I got near-perfect marks for them, but hearing *him* say it, causes a reaction in me that never would have happened if I still had my thirty-something-year-old, female teacher from last year.

"You've got a good eye," he tells me as he clicks a few more times. "I'm impressed."

I risk a glance at his face, and he's smiling at my work.

My breath gets caught in my throat. He's seriously the most gorgeous man I've ever seen.

"Which one is your favourite of this collection?" he questions me.

I reach for the mouse pad so I can find the image, but instead end up brushing his skin again.

He tugs his hand away and gently pushes my laptop back in my direction.

I can feel the blush on my cheeks, so I keep my head down as I click through the series, looking for the one image that has always stood out to me the most.

"That one," I say, and I hate the way my voice sounds. It's breathy and light and not at all strong and sure like the way I feel about my photos.

I peek up at him as he looks at my screen.

Trevor and Maddy are locked in an embrace and the night sky is almost magical above them. They look like they're the only two people left in the world.

He nods his head, his lip curling up again as though I've given him the answer he was hoping for. "I've got high expectations for you this semester, Perry."

I blush again as he passes by me and shifts his focus to Maddy, and it's not until class ends and I rise from my seat, that I realise he called me by my first name.

CHAPTER THREE

Liam

The last student files out of the room, and I rest my hands on my desk, my head falling forward as I breathe heavily.

I don't know what the fuck that was, but I've never felt a connection the way I did now.

Especially not to a woman who is probably close to ten years my junior.

Definitely not to a woman as off limits as a student.

I may have only been a teacher for this one day so far, but I'm fairly confident that thinking these kinds of thoughts is severely frowned upon, and acting on them is probably a fireable offence.

Being in the same room with her, in such close proximity was one hundred times more intense than the energy I felt this morning. It was overwhelming. I've never had to try so hard to keep my eyes *off* something.

"First class that rough, huh?"

My head snaps up and my gaze lands on Lincoln.

I cover my inner turmoil with a grin. "Something like that."

Lincoln has been my mate since we studied together at this very university.

He's the one who got me the job here – he's a graphics design lecturer, and when I found myself seeking a different lifestyle, he pulled some strings and got me this short-term gig.

"At least you've got mostly year threes. Those year ones, man, they test your patience."

I chuckle. "I'll have to remember that."

"If I get another jock that thinks design is going to be an easy ride to graduation, I think I might stick pins in my eyes."

I close my laptop and chuckle again. "My problem is another one entirely."

He strolls further into the room and frowns at me. "Are they an untalented bunch of losers or something?"

I shake my head. Sure, there were a few that are probably never going to make it in the industry, but as long as they work hard, I won't hold it against them. On the whole, there was enough potential... and then there was one student who was leaps and bounds above the others.

And of course, she has to be beautiful too.

"Can I ask you something, Linc? No judgement?"

He smirks. "You can ask me, but you know I'm gonna judge you."

I shake my head in amusement. It's probably the best offer I'm going to get as far as Linc is concerned.

"Were the girls this hot when we were at uni?"

He throws his head back and laughs. "Got yourself a sexy little student, have you?"

I blow out a deep breath. "I get the feeling the best answer here is, no comment."

"That's a tough break, man, happens to the best of us."

"Yeah?" I raise a brow at him. "You?"

He nods thoughtfully. "I've had a few, but none that have ever tempted me enough to risk losing my job – or my marriage for that matter."

No one is losing their job. Certainly not me, and definitely not because of a woman.

No matter how stunning she is.

I chuckle. "It's just a pretty girl, Linc, I'll survive – surely I can make it through my first week without getting the sack."

"Hey, I'll trade you for the meathead football players if you want?" he offers with a smirk.

I sling my bag over my shoulder and shake my head with a grin. "No deal."

I think I'll keep Perry Jenkins right where I can see her, even if she is firmly off limits.

I might not be allowed to touch, but there's nothing stopping me from looking.

It couldn't hurt, I tell myself.

I've got a sinking feeling that I might be singing a different tune by the end of the semester.

***

Well *fuck*.

This is the furthest thing from ideal.

When I set my senior class the task of planning a photoshoot three weeks ago, the last thing I expected was for Perry to offer to be her friend's model.

The sexy, yet tasteful boudoir-style shoot that Maddy has produced was even more of a surprise to me.

I've been in a state of semihardness for the past half an hour while I suggest edits to Maddy to enhance the images featuring her already flawless subject.

I'd been doing so well too, other than allowing myself to call the students by their first names after my slip up on day one, I haven't got any closer.

I still find my gaze wandering to Perry every few minutes, but I catch myself quickly now. The draw is just as strong, if not stronger, but I've never been one to give in easily.

But seeing these images, some of which she's virtually naked in, I can feel my resolve slipping.

"I'd re-shoot that one." I point to possibly the most seductive of the lot. "Lower the lighting and adjust your angle so it's more in line with these." I point to a series of another few images.

"Alright, prof – *Mr. Conrad*." Maddy scrawls down the notes I've just given her and smiles brightly at me.

I resist the urge to smirk.

I've heard the nickname she's given me circulating through the room, but I pretend I don't.

That girl is trouble with a capital 'T'.

"And this one here, I'd get her legs opened just a fraction wider," I say, even though the words shouldn't be coming out of my mouth.

"You hear that, P? You gotta open those sexy legs for me." She winks at Perry.

Jesus Christ.

That was *not* what I needed to hear, not about Perry.

All I can think about is this beautiful woman beneath me, wearing that sexy black lace, her legs open and waiting.

It's wrong on so many levels.

So, *so* many.

"It's official, I'm never modelling for you again," Perry announces, her cheeks flaming red.

She catches my eye, and I give her a small smile. "How is your shoot coming along, Perry?"

I step away from Maddy and her album of temptation and look at the screen in front of Perry.

She quickly closes a window and brings up another album.

"What was that?" I question.

She shakes her head. "Nothing."

"It didn't look like nothing."

"Sorry, it's not for my project, I probably shouldn't have been working on it in class."

I don't blame her for working on something else. Her assignment is already perfectly executed. She barely had to do any editing to her work – she's got a real gift for capturing natural light flawlessly.

Clearly, she isn't distracted by my presence the same way I am by hers. Where I feel like I'm constantly behind the eight ball, she's well and truly on top of things.

I drag a spare stool over and sit next to her.

"Can I see?" I ask softly.

She looks at me, her brows raised and her teeth nibbling on her bottom lip.

"Alright," she whispers. "But it's not finished, and I'm having trouble with it, so don't judge too harshly."

"Just show me."

She looks like she wants to say something more but doesn't.

She clicks the minimised Photoshop tab and the image appears on the screen.

Woah.

It's seriously good.

She's captured a couple holding an umbrella in the rain, and their reflection is in the puddle on the ground in front of them.

It's a beautiful shot, but there's something more to it that I can't put my finger on, there's a depth and real sense of emotion that can't be scripted.

"Candid or posed?" I murmur.

"Candid," she replies, and I can hear the nerves in her voice. "I was walking to the studio one afternoon last year and it just caught my eye. The couple were having such an intense moment, I couldn't just walk by... the rain, the water, it was all just a fluke."

Taking a shot like this was no fluke, it was a good eye and talent.

"I showed them the raw images afterwards, and they were happy for me to work on them – I got their email addresses," she adds hurriedly, as though I might have thought she took these photos without permission.

I ignore her rambling.

"It's a really good shot. Have you got others?"

She nods and pulls up a file. She clicks through each shot, and I seriously can't believe her skill level.

She could walk out of this class now, without graduating and do a better job than half of the industry professionals I've worked with in my career.

She goes back to the image she's working on and shrugs her shoulders.

"This is the best of the bunch, but there's something not right about it. I can't put my finger on it."

I see what she means; it's a great shot, but the finished project could be better. It's something that no one else in this class would even notice, but Perry isn't on the same playing field as the others, and I think everyone in this room knows that.

"I think I might have an idea that could help..."

"Yeah?" Her eyes light up with excitement.

"Yeah." I nod. "But since it's not a requirement project, I can't really work on it with you during class."

I don't know what the hell I'm thinking, I can feel the offer coming up my throat, an offer I *shouldn't* be making given the attraction I feel towards this woman, but it's too late now, I can't stop myself.

"But if you want to get together during study break or after classes, I'd be happy to help then."

She bites down on her lip again, and I have to really work to pull my eyes from her mouth.

"That would be amazing, thank you, Mr. Conrad."

"I have a free period next," I tell her, continuing to punish myself.

"So do I," she whispers.

I nod my head. "Well then... you're on."

Shit.

I guess this is really happening then.

CHAPTER FOUR

Perry

I sit nervously at my desk as the other students file out of the room.

I'm so on edge, it's *insane*. I don't know what freaks me out more, the idea of being alone with Mr. Conrad, or the thought of him getting up close and personal with my work again.

Maddy shuts her laptop with a loud thud, and I jump.

"I can't believe you have a date with that sexy-ass man," she whispers.

I shush her. "It's not a date," I hiss. "It's a tutor session you psycho."

She giggles. "Oh yeah, I'm sure you'd be this worked up about a tutor session with Mrs. Oliver." She raises her brows at me knowingly.

I scowl at her.

I probably *would* be worked up about spending time one on one with the sculpture lecturer we had in year one who looked like she didn't own a hairbrush and smelt like feet, but not for the same reasons.

Obviously.

Mrs. Oliver didn't make my heart race and my palms sweat.

Mr. Conrad certainly does.

I glance back up at him. He's wiping something off the board – his back to us, his broad shoulders straining against the fabric of his blue shirt.

She makes kissing noises as she catches me staring.

I shove her towards the door, and she shakes her head in amusement.

"Good luck."

"As long as I make it out of here without calling him that stupid nickname you've got stuck in my head, I'll be happy," I hiss at her as she smirks at me deviously.

"See ya later, Mr. Conrad," she calls to him, and he turns and waves a hand at her.

He watches her leave the room and then it's just the two of us.

His eyes find mine and he smiles before dipping his gaze to the floor.

If I didn't know better, I'd swear he was as nervous as I am.

His smile grows as he turns away from me, back to the board.

He's got the sexiest dimple in his left cheek, and it is *not* helping this situation in the slightest.

I really, *really* want his help with my photos. I may or may not have looked up his work online, and it's *incredible*, but I have to be able to focus, and not make a blithering idiot out of myself for that to happen, and I'm not sure I'm capable anymore.

I'm a complete cliché right now – the student crushing on her teacher, but *shit*, I bet no one would blame me when he looks like that.

He is *gorgeous*.

"You all ready to go with that image?"

I nod quickly and use one of my shaky hands to bring it up on the screen in front of me.

I study it again and frown.

"I don't know what it is, but I just can't get it perfect."

He drags out the stool next to me and sits down.

The fabric covering his broad shoulder brushes my arm, and I have to remind myself that I'm an adult now, and I can be near a man without getting butterflies in my stomach.

The scent of his cologne wafts past my nose, and I inhale deeply.

"I think you're being too hard on yourself, it's a really good image."

"Thank you," I whisper, my cheeks flaming with his praise.

I hate that I'm blushing. I'm not the blushing girl, not normally anyway.

"So why don't you tell me what you don't like about it and we'll go from there."

I sneak a look up at him, and he smiles at me encouragingly.

I glance back at the screen, my head tipping to the side as I study my work.

I point at a section on the image. "This isn't right, and over here..." I shift my focus. "This just needs to be sharper, or more defined..."

I'm rambling total nonsense.

I nibble on my bottom lip as I think about what I'm trying to say.

"Right now, I just feel like the focus is on the image as a whole, and not just the couple... They're the reason I took the photo in the first place. They should be the main point... Does that make sense?"

"It makes perfect sense." I see him nod out of the corner of my eye.

I sigh. "No matter what I try, it never seems to work."

"Do you want to know what I'd do?" he asks, and I can't help but look right at him.

It hits me again, just how close we are.

This feels like dangerous territory given how out of control my hormones seem to be when he's around.

"Please," I say, and honestly, I'm not sure what I'm asking him for anymore.

He looks at me, his blue eyes lingering just a little too long before he darts them back to the screen.

I let out a breath as he releases me from his spell.

"Well to be honest," he says, seemingly unaware to the reaction he's evoking in me, "I'd probably crop out their heads."

"What?" I demand, his outrageous suggestion pulling me from my lust-filled haze. "Cut their heads off? Are you high?"

He chuckles and the deep sound reverberates through every damn inch of my body.

I slap a hand over my mouth.

I did *not* just say that.

Oh dear god, I think I just asked my lecturer if he was high...

"Sorry, I didn't mean to ask that, Mr. Conrad, seriously, it's just an expression."

His chuckle deepens. "It's all good, and call me Liam, let's keep this casual, we're not in class anymore."

Oh *lord*. Liam. Even his name is hot.

"And I'm not high, I promise. But seriously, crop out their heads and see."

I eye him sceptically, but do as he's asked, readjusting the image so their heads are cut off.

"Go even further, take it down to their lower legs."

I frown, but do what he's told me, and as I make the final click, I see exactly what he's trying to get me to achieve.

The couple's image is reflected in the puddle on the ground, and now that the crystal-clear image has been cropped out, all the focus is on the reflection.

It's beautiful.

"A few adjustments on that, and I think you'll have what you're after."

"Huh," I muse, clicking my tongue.

I almost feel stupid for not seeing it myself.

I'd been so focused on the couple that I overlooked the beauty of the rest of my shot.

"It was so simple."

"Sometimes something can be right there in front of you, but you don't see it for what it is... you think you want one thing, but it turns out to be something else."

I glance at him and find him watching me again.

I don't know if we're still talking about photos or not.

"Thank you... *Liam*," I say softly.

His eyes flutter closed momentarily as his name falls from my lips.

I can feel myself leaning in towards him, and I can't make it stop, I'm drawn to him in a way I can't even begin to understand or explain.

He leans in a little closer, and I'm almost tempted to pinch myself, because I must be fucking dreaming right now.

"Hey, Liam, you wanna get a coffee?" A voice behind me startles us both, and I pull away abruptly.

I glance at the door and see one of the other lecturers stroll in.

His eyes land on us for the first time, and I thank the stars above that he didn't walk in without announcing his presence first, or he'd be taking in a very different scene.

"Shit, sorry, I thought you'd be alone," he says. "I'll come back."

It's Mr. Radcliff, my graphics design teacher from first year.

He's not too hard on the eye either. I'm sure he gets his fair share of unwanted student attention, but he doesn't hold a flame to the man sitting next to me.

"It's all good, Linc, I'm just helping Perry with a project."

Mr. Radcliff studies me carefully, as though he can't quite figure me out, and I shift uncomfortably in my seat under his intense scrutiny.

"You were in one of my classes, right?" he finally asks.

I nod. "First year."

"I remember you; you had a good eye."

"Um... thanks."

"I told you." Liam shrugs.

He turns his attention to his co-worker. "I'm going to be here for a while, I'll catch you after work? I thought you might be keen for a workout."

I hold back a groan. Now I've got a visual of the two of them in gym shorts, pushing weights or doing whatever it is that hot guys do at gyms that make them so hot.

Mr. Radcliff still hasn't answered him, and when I glance back, I don't miss the warning look he's giving Liam.

He sees me looking and softens. "Yeah, sure, I'll see you at the gym. Six o'clock?"

"Sounds good," Liam replies, turning his back on the man still lingering in the doorway.

I smile awkwardly and follow his lead, turning back to my work.

"Sorry about that," Liam says a few moments later.

I shrug. "I'm sorry you're missing out on coffee; I owe you one."

He chuckles. "Careful, I might hold you to that."

I bite down on my lip to stop from smiling too wide, all the while hoping that he'll do exactly that.

CHAPTER FIVE

Liam

I had a feeling that an interrogation was coming, so when it does, I'm prepared for it at least.

"She's the hot one you told me about, isn't she?"

He's grinning, but I can see the underlying hint of wariness in his eyes.

He's concerned for me, and I can't even fault him on that.

I'm concerned for me.

I don't know what the hell I was thinking earlier, but I'm pretty sure if he hadn't have walked into that room when he did, I would have found myself kissing a student, right there on the campus.

Images of her in black lace underwear swirl through my brain as I consider lying to him, but I can't do it, Linc has been my best mate for a long time now, and even if I did lie, he'd probably see right through it in thirty seconds flat and call me on it even quicker.

"Yeah, she's the fucking hot one alright," I grunt as I tug on the laces of my gym shoes.

"I see what you mean."

I nod, but don't look at him. I know he's not done yet.

He's got me through a lot this past year, and we've learnt to hear what the other *isn't* saying.

"You two looked pretty cosy."

I grimace, then do my best to drop the emotion from my face before I look at him again. "I've barely said two words to her, she was having trouble with an edit, so I gave her some pointers. Nothing I wouldn't have done for any other student in my class."

It's a half lie. I doubt I would have offered for anyone else, but I wouldn't have turned down a request either.

"She's got skills if I remember rightly?"

I stand up and walk towards the weights bench. I need to keep myself busy or he's going to figure out just how messed up I am about this girl.

I don't even want to admit to *myself* how much I've been thinking about her, let alone to him.

"She's the best photographer in her year by a country mile."

"Shit," he mutters, and I turn and frown at him.

"What?"

"You always had a thing for chicks with talent."

I brush his comment off with a laugh. "What, as opposed to having a thing for chicks with no talent?"

"You know what I mean," he presses, "I bet you're as hot for her photographs as you are for her."

"I am *not* hot for her. She's my student. She'd be what, twenty years old?"

"Could even still be nineteen," he replies, and it hits me like a whack of reality to the balls.

I'm twenty-*nine* years old, and while that might be considerably younger than most of the members of staff at the university, it's a hell of a lot older than nineteen.

I might be fantasising about a teenager.

I don't even want to think about how fucking disgusting that makes me.

I must look as sick as I feel because he claps me on the shoulder.

"I'm just saying is all, looking is one thing, but crossing that line is something you might not be able to come back from – and not just because you're her teacher."

I shake my head. "I don't need a warning, bro, I'm not dumb enough to get involved with *anyone*, let alone a student."

I'm not sure *I* even believe what I'm saying.

He nods his head and chuckles. "She sure is pretty though."

"Don't remind me," I mutter under my breath as I stack a few extra weights on either end of the bar.

Apparently, I'm in the mood to punish myself in more ways than one.

***

I'm making a few adjustments to a slideshow when movement catches the corner of my eye.

My heart starts doing that stupid fucking erratic slamming against my ribcage when my brain registers who it is.

For the love of god, I really need to get a grip. Being back here in this environment is fucking with my head. It's like I'm a teenager all over again, but this time around, I've got responsibilities, people who depend on me.

"Morning," she says, a beautiful smile playing on her lips. "You're early."

The tone in my voice is far too pleased, but that's what she does to me. I can't hide it. I've never been very good at hiding my emotions – I've never had to before now.

She holds out a takeaway coffee cup. "As promised."

I grin. "You got me coffee?"

She nods and takes another step closer. "Yip, and it's the good stuff, I promise."

I chuckle and take it from her. I sip it, and I don't know how, but it's exactly how I take it.

I glance at her in question and she smirks victoriously.

"The chick that works there knew exactly how the hot teacher likes it."

Her eyes widen and her cheeks stain with blush when she realises what she's just said.

I smirk over the rim of my cup before I take another sip.

She clears her throat awkwardly and pulls her eyes from me as she strolls back towards her spot in the classroom.

I hate the whispers I hear in the halls about my looks and the unwanted attention I get from the female students, but it's different when it comes from Perry's lips – it's not unwanted in the slightest when she's the one thinking it.

"So... Mr. Conrad –"

"Liam," I interrupt her before I can even think about it.

She turns sharply, one of her brows raised. "It's nearly time for class," she argues.

I shrug and keep on digging myself into this hole that is already well above my head. "Nearly isn't here yet."

She watches me for a few beats. "Do you still get your camera out?"

"Whenever I can. I'm actually planning to head up Rocky Hill on Saturday to get some shots."

"Rocky Hill?" she asks, her brow furrowed.

I nod. "It's about an hour inland. The view up there is incredible. You can catch the sunrise first thing, or clear uninterrupted stars at night."

"Sounds pretty."

"It's beautiful. Not too many people know about it. You can see for miles."

She looks back at me and smiles, her dark wavy hair falling around her face.

"You should come with me." The words are out of my mouth and settling in the air between us before I can even consider what I've just offered.

Her eyebrows shoot up in surprise and her mouth falls open a fraction.

This isn't a teacher volunteering to help a student, and we both know it.

This is me inviting her because I want to share it with her.

"*Me*?" she questions.

I should back out now, say it's not appropriate and apologise for making the suggestion in the first place, but my brain can't get the signal to my mouth. It's taken on a mind of its own. "Yeah." I nod. "*Come*, you could get some amazing shots for your end-of-year piece."

She scrunches up her nose. "You think that would be okay... you know, with the university?"

My moral compass is so far bent right now because when I smirk at her and say, "What they don't know won't hurt them," I don't even feel bad about it.

CHAPTER SIX

Perry

This is the worst idea I've ever had.

Sneaking out of my house at five in the morning so I can go on a field trip with my teacher, who is also the sexiest man I've ever met, can't lead to *anything* good.

I'm bound to make a fool of myself with this stupid crush; it's definitely going to happen... I just have to hope he'll be gentle with me when it does.

I shouldn't even be going, but when those blue eyes of his looked into mine and he said it would be our little secret, I was a complete goner.

I was giving him my address before I even registered what the hell I was doing.

A silver station wagon pulls up at the curb, the passenger window rolls down, and there he is.

I release the breath I'd been holding at the sight of him.

It doesn't seem like such a bad idea now that he's here.

I'm so totally screwed.

He smiles at me as I approach, and my belly flutters.

I grip my camera case a little tighter and glance back over my shoulder at my still-darkened house.

Maddy and Trevor are sleeping, probably will be for hours. That made my escape easy, but I've got no idea what I'm going to tell her when I get back later.

I told *no one* where I was going.

It probably isn't the wisest move, given that we're virtual strangers, and this is like the part of the movie where everyone yells at the girl, 'don't get in the car with a stranger, are you stupid?' But maybe I am stupid, because I feel like I can trust him.

I'm still not sure if he was kidding about keeping this only between us, but I did. Just to be safe.

Besides, if I told Maddy where I was going, she would have made a *massive* deal out of it.

Sure, right now, as I reach for the door handle of his car, it feels like a pretty big deal after all, but she would have made it out to be something it's not – some sexy, forbidden affair.

It's not like that – no matter how much I fantasise about it being *exactly* like that.

"Good morning," he says as I slip into the warm interior of his car. His voice is husky and hoarse, and I love the idea that I might be the first person to get to hear it today. It makes me feel special, in a delusional, I'm-crushing-on-my-teacher kind of way.

"*Hey*," I breathe.

I talked myself into thinking I wouldn't be nervous, but those are just wasted hours I won't ever get back because I'm *freaking* out now that I'm so close to him again.

He presses a button and the window rolls back up.

"Sorry it's so early."

I click on my seatbelt, and he pulls out into the empty street.

"I don't mind early, try keeping me up all night and you'll have problems though."

"Noted." He grins, and I honestly could die.

I can't believe I just said that.

As if he needs to worry about keeping me awake all hours of the night. Jesus, I don't know what the hell is wrong with me.

"You alright to stop for coffee in the next town over?"

He looks a bit guilty about asking, but I'm not an idiot, I know it'll get people talking if we were to arrive at the café around the corner together – no matter how innocent it is. And besides, it's not like it's open at this hour of the morning anyway.

"Sounds perfect."

He nods his head, a smile tugging at his lips.

"Have you always lived around here?" he asks as we drive through the still-sleeping town.

I shake my head. "Nah, I'm from a little town a few hours south. I've been here since first year though, and I love it. The winters are a little warmer than back home, so that's a bonus."

"It gets colder than this?" he asks with a mock shudder.

I laugh. "I take it you're from somewhere warm?"

He chuckles. "I'm actually born and bred near where we're headed right now, but I've spent years travelling the globe, and I always gravitated towards the sun. This winter has been a shock to the system."

I think I'd be the same. I love warm weather. Islands and beaches.

"That photoshoot you did in Greece was incredible."

He glances at me in surprise before looking back at the road. "You looked up my work?"

I nod, unashamed about my blatant stalking. I'm not at all embarrassed about looking at his work. What I *am* embarrassed about is staring at that dimple and his sexy smile when I shouldn't be. Not to mention the fact that I've spent half of our classes fantasising about the body he hides under those button-downs.

I'm also pretty embarrassed about the dream I had last night, the one where I found myself pinned against a soft mattress, my body naked beneath his.

"If you've uploaded a photo to the internet, I'm fairly confident I've seen it," I confirm.

He chuckles. "*Thorough.*"

It wasn't hard to find. His website is professional and up to date and he's well known in this country's photography community.

He's won numerous awards for his work and, other than those awards and his photographs, there wasn't a single thing to find about him on Google.

As disappointing as that was for me on a Friday night, half a pizza deep into my stalk session, it was good to know that he didn't have some big scandal following him around like so many people do these days.

"Why'd you decide to teach instead of do?" I ask the question that's been bugging me for weeks now.

He's obviously still so passionate about photography, and his eye is impeccably good, yet he's stuck in a classroom teaching people like me instead of really using his talent.

"It was just time for a change," he replies. I feel like there's more he's not saying, but I'm not about to attempt to delve into his personal life. It's not my business.

I know nothing about him. He could even be married for all I know – as sick as that idea makes me feel.

I glance at his left hand. There's no wedding band. I almost laugh at myself for checking again, as though I didn't do exactly that on the very first day of class.

No ring, no wife.

That was another dream entirely; we snuck off to this mystery location of his, and just when he was about to kiss me, his wife turned up, screaming her head off.

That was a fun one. *Not*.

I much prefer the first of the two.

God, I'm seriously deluded.

"Is Mr. Radcliff a friend of yours?" I ask, thinking back to the day he found us working together in the studio.

"Lincoln... *yeah*, we studied together. Obviously, we went down different paths in third year, but we've stayed close. He's the one who got me the job. He'd been teaching for about five years already."

"Yeah, I remember him... I had him in first year."

"Yeah, you mentioned that... how'd you find him?"

"It was good, he knows what he's talking about. Didn't take any shit from the jocks that used to muck around up the back." I grin.

He chuckles. "It sounds like it must be Groundhog Day for him then."

I giggle. "I bet. I don't know what it is about photography and design, but those sporty guys that don't want to be in class seem to think they're going to get an easy ride."

"You play sport?" he questions.

I shake my head furiously. "*Nope*. I don't have a whole lot of that hand-eye co-ordination that is kinda required. Do you?"

"Not so much anymore. I played basketball when I was at uni."

"Were you good?" I settle deeper into my seat and realise that I've twisted my body so that I'm facing him.

I don't know when I got so comfortable, but I am. My nerves have all but disappeared.

"I was alright, Linc was better. He played a season for the national team after we graduated."

It's sweet, hearing the pride in his voice as he brags about his friend.

"Go Mr. Radcliff." I grin.

His smile deepens and the dimple I'm growing so fond of appears.

I really want to ask him what year he graduated, so I can gauge how old he is, but I can't do it, it feels too personal, and there's also the fact that I'm a complete chicken shit.

He gets in first anyway, asking me question after question until we settle into a rhythm of taking turns, finding out little things about one another.

I've finally built up the courage to ask his age when he flicks his indicator on, and the car begins to slow.

I glance at the time on the clock, we've been travelling for half an hour already, and I have no idea where that time went.

He pulls into a park and runs his hand through his light brown hair, ruffling it on the top.

"We're about halfway," he says with a shy smile, his eyes slowly raking over my face.

"Okay," I whisper, my nerves coming back full force.

It's different when he's looking at me. When those gorgeous blue eyes were staring off out the windscreen, it was easier to feel at ease, but not now.

Not at all.

Now I feel off kilter.

"You want to get that coffee?" He tips his head across the street to a sleepy little café.

"If you expect me to remember how to use my camera, I think that might be a good idea."

He chuckles and dips his head in that way he does. It makes me think he's shy, but he can't be. Not around *me*.

I can't handle his eyes on me, but at the same time, the minute they're gone from mine, I miss them.

He opens his door and I do the same. We walk silently, side by side, stealing glances at one another like two strangers who share a secret.

***

"This is it."

"Holy shit," I breathe as I lean forward to try and see further up into the sky. "You weren't kidding about needing sensible shoes."

He chuckles. "Yeah, it's a bit of a hike."

"Will we make sunrise?"

He glances at his watch. "*Maybe*... if we move fast. It looks like a long way up, but it should only take about twenty minutes, half an hour maybe."

I get the feeling it would take him a hell of a lot less, but me on the other hand, I'll probably take half the day.

He parks the car in the middle of nowhere and turns off the head lights.

"Did you bring a jacket?"

I nod, reaching onto the floor and holding up the thick winter jacket I brought with me.

I've also got enough snacks to feed a small army, enough water to last a few days and every camera lens I own.

I'm nothing if not prepared.

He climbs out of the car and I follow suit.

I shrug on my jacket and do my best to swing my huge backpack onto my back without making it look like an effort.

I reach back in for my camera bag and nearly topple over.

I hear his deep laugh behind me. "You planning to camp out for a week or something?"

I straighten up and smirk at him. "You won't be making fun of me when we got lost and have to survive on our own."

He laughs, the throaty noise swallowing me whole and wrapping around my heart like a vice.

It's official. This was a really, really bad idea.

And not because I think we're actually going to get lost, or because I'm worried he's going to murder me and dump my body out here in the middle of nowhere, but because I'm feeling things I shouldn't be.

Feelings that have no place between a student and her teacher.

Feelings that would probably see me kicked out of university if I acted on them, not to mention severely humiliated when he shot me down.

His hand lands gently on my shoulder. "At least let me carry it then."

I open my mouth to argue, but he's already slipping the strap down my arm.

Even through my thick jacket, I've got goosebumps where he's touching me.

"Seriously, Perry, you can't walk up that hill with *that* bag, not if we want to get up there and back today."

"Fine," I whisper, my protest weak at best.

I've always been a sucker for a gentleman, and if he wants to carry my bag, I'm going to damn well let him.

He tugs it from my back, and honestly, I'm glad it's gone, that thing weighed a tonne.

He slings it over his shoulder like it's no big deal at all.

It's still pretty dark, but I can make him out in the shadows.

He strolls around to his boot, so I follow. He gets out a blanket and his camera gear.

I take the blanket from him, he narrows his eyes at me, but doesn't argue.

"Lead the way, tour guide," I announce with a grin.

He hands me a head lamp before slamming his boot shut and locking his car.

I didn't even think about bringing a torch. I didn't think about the fact that it would be dark at all.

I'm the girl who thinks she's prepared but finds herself deep into the wilderness with nothing she actually needs.

"Oh thanks." I smile gratefully. Maybe I'll have a shot at making it up there without twisting an ankle if I can actually see where I'm going.

I try to slip it onto my head but fail miserably. I'm not outdoorsy at all, and I've never worn one of these before.

He steps in front of me, and my hands start to shake, which only makes it harder to do what I'm trying to do.

"Let me do it for you," he says softly.

I pass it to him and let my trembling hands fall to my sides. I stand dead still, not moving a muscle as he adjusts the strap and reaches for my head.

He gently brushes some hair from my face, and I find myself glancing up to look at his expression.

He's focusing so hard, his fingers still lingering on my skin.

I'm barely breathing, I'm scared if I move it'll remind him that it's *me*, and that he's meant to keep his distance.

He slides the strap around my head, and it fits snugly.

"There," he murmurs, his eyes shifting down to meet my gaze.

His hands are still in my hair, tenderly grasping my head.

We're so close to one another, it wouldn't take anything at all to come together.

I can imagine how soft his lips would feel, how the rough stubble on his face would scratch against me...

"We should get going," he says softly, and I nod.

We *definitely* should.

Before I do something really, really stupid.

CHAPTER SEVEN

Liam

I stay at least half a metre in front of her the entire time we hike up this damn hill.

I don't trust myself to get any closer than that, not after the moment we shared when we arrived.

I could have kissed her.

I really fucking wanted to kiss her.

I probably would have kissed my teaching career goodbye too.

It was reckless and stupid and all I can think about doing is making it happen all over again, but going through with it this time, not backing out like some pussy who is too afraid to go after what he wants.

I glance over my shoulder and watch as her chest heaves with the exertion, my resolve weakening more with each moment I look at her.

Going through with it is *exactly* what I need to do.

I need to find my balls, forget about my job – forget about everything else and follow my heart.

I want Perry.

I've been denying myself for *weeks* now, but it hasn't made the fact any less true.

I. Want. Her.

I want to know what food she likes; I want to know what side of the bed she sleeps on, I want to know what she looks like when she shoots a photo, and what she'd look like when I shot a photo of her.

I want to know how her lips would feel against mine, and how her body would respond when I touched it.

I want to know *everything* and I'm not going to lie to myself about it for a second longer.

I can't do it anymore.

This past year has taught me that life is short. It's *so* fucking short and it can be taken from you in a heartbeat.

I owe it to myself not to ignore this, because I've *never* felt this way, and given everything I've been through, that's saying a lot.

I take another few steps and heave myself and this ridiculous backpack she brought with her up the final step of the trail.

I stand and watch Perry following behind me. She's so beautiful it hurts to look at her.

"Screw it," I mutter to myself, making my decision – consequences be damned.

I reach my hand out to help her up, and she looks at me in surprise. I've kept my distance the whole walk and now suddenly, the rules have changed.

"I've got you," I tell her, my voice sounding raspy and strained.

She places her hand delicately in mine, and I tug her up the final step.

The sun is just beginning to rise, and she gasps as her feet land in front of me and she sees what I'm seeing.

Only, she's not seeing *exactly* what I'm seeing, because I'm seeing all of this *and* her.

I must have been here at least a dozen times in my life, but it has never, ever, looked this perfect.

"Oh my god, it's beautiful," she breathes.

She's right about that. I've never seen anything like it.

Her dark eyes wander over the rocky cliff top and out to the horizon.

I reach up and turn off my light and then do the same to hers.

My hand lingers near her face and it's only then that I realise I'm still holding her other hand in mine.

I cup her jaw in my hand and hear her gasp softly as she finally looks up at me.

I don't know what she sees in my eyes, but whatever it is, she doesn't pull away, in fact she steps in closer, her free hand pressing against my chest.

I think we both see the line we're about to cross.

"*Perry*," I breathe.

"Are you sure about this, Liam?" she whispers.

If I wasn't before, I would have been now, hearing her say my name in that sexy voice.

"I've just got *one* question," I murmur.

She waits for me to ask it.

"How old are you?"

"Twenty," she whispers quickly.

"Twenty is better than nineteen," I growl.

I dip my head and brush my lips against hers.

She gasps again, and I swallow it, kissing her more fervently than before.

I drop her hand and grasp her face with both my hands. She wraps her arm around my middle and tugs me closer, her lips moving against mine with a hunger I could never have predicted.

Sunlight tries to force its way through my closed lids, and I pull away.

She breathes heavily, and I rest my forehead against hers. "We're missing the view."

"I don't care." She sighs.

I chuckle. "I didn't bring you all the way up here for this."

She drags her bottom lip into her mouth and looks up at me, uncertainty in her eyes.

"We can do this anywhere," I whisper, "anytime."

As much as I want to keep kissing her, I don't want to miss my shot.

She nods, and I somehow find the strength to pull away.

I reach for my bag and unzip it before clipping my lens to my camera. She does the same.

"Will you do something for me?" I ask her nervously.

She nods, her expression shy.

"Will you let me take your photo?"

Her eyes widen. "You want to take *my* photo?"

"More than anything in the world," I tell her honestly as the sun inches higher in the sky.

I raise my camera and wait for her to give me permission.

"Okay," she finally says.

I click the shutter.

***

"Just one more."

She giggles and I take yet another photo of her smiling face.

"You said that two hours ago."

"I lied."

"No shit." She smirks, and fuck it, I snap a picture of that too.

I've got enough material here to last a lifetime. I'm trying to stop, I really am, but then she does something else, and I *have* to have that moment captured for all of eternity as well.

I've even got photos of her taking photos.

She looks exactly how I imagined she would with a camera in her hand.

Serene, *happy* – she looks like she was born for it.

"C'mon, click, give it up already."

"Click?" I question with a frown.

She rolls her eyes. "Yeah, *click*, because all I've got from you is the click, click, click of that damn shutter, all morning."

She laughs, and I chuckle. I want to kiss that mouth again so badly.

We haven't talked about our kiss or what it means, for now at least, while we're out here all alone, it doesn't matter.

We're just two people who feel something for one another.

Two people who are in no hurry to get back to the real world.

"I'm going to get some snacks out, and if you try and take photos of me eating, there is going to be trouble," she warns me as she sits down on the blanket that I've laid out for us.

"What if I like trouble?" I question, but I lower my lens as she reaches for her huge bag.

She smirks. "I think I've figured that out already, *Mr. Conrad*."

I set my gear down and prowl towards her. "It's going to be like that, is it?"

She shrugs, a mischievous glint in her eye. "*Maybe.*"

I drop to my knees in between her legs, and she's laid flat on her back with me hovering over her in a flash.

A breathy sigh falls from her lips, and I'd give just about anything to hear that sound again.

I don't know what it is about this woman that drives me so crazy, but I know one thing, I've *never* felt like this before, and finally kissing her has only intensified that.

I lower my face to hers, teasing her with soft brushes of my lips against her cheeks, jawline, neck, the smattering of freckles across her nose and even her eye lids.

"I love these freckles."

"*Liam*," she whispers, and I can't hold back a moment longer.

I lower myself onto her, supporting my weight on my elbows.

She pushes up and captures my bottom lip between her teeth, and I moan before melding my lips to hers in a flurry of passion and heat.

I don't know what the hell we're going to do when we go back, because I can't give her up, not now that I've had a taste.

I run my hand down her side, and she giggles softly against my mouth.

"What's the matter, babe, you ticklish?" I chuckle.

"No." She fixes her face into a serious expression.

I slide my hand lower and she cracks again, giggling and squirming beneath me.

"Stop," she cries, the sound echoing into the valley beneath us.

I chuckle and slide down, so my face is level with her rib cage.

I lift her layers until my fingers brush her bare skin. I can feel her heart pounding and I grin to myself.

She's *definitely* feeling this too.

I press my lips against her bare flesh, and she shudders.

Her hands find my head and wind into my hair, tugging firmly.

I don't know if she's trying to pull me away or hold me close.

I kiss a trail from her rib cage to the waistband of her jeans, and back up again.

She's so responsive, from her breathy moans to the goose-bumps on her skin.

It's easy to forget why this is a bad idea when she's like this. That's how utterly dangerous she is.

I glance up at her, her dark eyes are focused solely on me, her mouth parted slightly in pleasure.

She blushes when our eyes meet, and I grin. I love that blush.

She tugs on my hair, pulling me to her, and I follow her lead until our mouths meet again.

I kiss her until I'm breathless and beside myself with need.

I haven't been this hard in what feels like forever, and my need to sink deep inside her is growing by the second.

I need to cool this down before I take her right here on top of Rocky Hill like some kind of horny teenager.

I pull back and brush a dark strand of hair from her face.

She's breathing heavy, her dark eyes burning bright with desire.

It's really fucking hard to do the right thing when she's looking at me like that.

"Are you okay?" she whispers, her hand coming up to stroke my jaw.

I blow out a breath. "I'm just thinking about what happens next."

She nods in understanding. "Nothing has to happen if you don't want it to."

I roll off her and onto my back. I run my hand through my hair in frustration before sitting up.

She sits up next to me.

"That's the problem, Perry, I really fucking want it to happen, rules be damned."

I reach for her hand and she offers it to me willingly, our fingers intertwining effortlessly, like they've done it a thousand times.

"That's what I was hoping you'd say," she whispers, and my heart rate increases.

She climbs into my lap, straddling me, and it's the sexiest thing I've ever seen. Even layered up in warm clothing, she's an absolute vixen.

"It still doesn't help the reality of our situation though, does it?"

Her arms are around my neck, her fingers playing with the hair at the back of my head, and mine are wrapped around her middle, holding her tight like I'm afraid she might disappear, because frankly, I am.

"We'll figure something out," she reassures me. "It'll be our little secret, just like today."

"I can't ask you to hide from the world, Perry, I don't want to turn you into a liar."

Because if we were to do this, that's exactly what would happen.

She'd have to lie to her friends – we both would.

We'd have to sneak around and hide from everyone.

That's not the kind of relationship I want.

A woman like Perry deserves to be shown off to the world, not hidden away like a dirty little secret.

"It'd be worth it for *you*."

My heart swells in my chest.

"I can't go back to pretending I don't feel this," she says softly, her eyes probing mine. "I'd rather have you in secret than not have you at all."

I nod my head. I feel the same way – as wrong as it is.

We stare at each other for a long moment, soaking in the freedom we have right now.

"I've just got one question," she says, mirroring my earlier phrasing.

"What is it?"

"How old are you?"

I grin. "I'm twenty-nine."

She smirks and shrugs a shoulder. "Twenty-nine is better than thirty."

I chuckle, a deep throaty laugh that comes from right inside me.

This might be wrong as far as the rules, morals, and ethics go, but for me, nothing has felt this right in a long time.

CHAPTER EIGHT

Perry

I float into the classroom like I've taken up residence on a cloud, miles above the planet.

Every moment since I got into Liam's car has felt so surreal.

I've just got to get through this class without undressing him with my eyes and then tonight I get to see him in private. Maybe I'll even get to do some real undressing if I'm lucky.

I still can't figure out how I've found myself in the position every female student – and even some of the males – want to be in, but here I am.

"Are you even listening to me?" Maddy demands, dragging me from my fantasy world and slamming me right back down to earth.

"Sorry, *what*?" I ask as I land eyes on the beautiful man at the front.

"I asked if you were going to be home tonight, we're making pizza for dinner."

I shake my head. "Sorry, I'm going out, you'll have the place to yourselves."

"Where are you sneaking off to this time?" She raises a brow at me sassily.

"I'm *not* sneaking off," I grumble.

Liam turns as we take our seats, his gorgeous blue eyes seeking me out for no more than a few seconds, but somehow saying so much in the short time.

My heart rate picks up, as it always seems to whenever he's around, and I attempt futilely to slow it down.

I don't know what I'm going to tell Maddy about where I'm going tonight when she questions me further, because she will. She's the nosiest person I know.

She didn't miss the fact that I was gone all day over the weekend, and I felt bad for lying to her, but it rolled so naturally off my tongue when the time came.

I told her that I got up early to photograph the sunrise and then spent the day working on various school projects.

I guess it was *somewhat* true. I just neglected to mention the company I kept, and I certainly didn't tell her about all the hot makeout sessions.

Liam didn't bring me home until after dark, but it still didn't feel like long enough with him.

He's addictive in the best way, or maybe it's the worst way given our situation – I still haven't decided yet.

I pull my laptop from my bag and set it down on the table.

I can feel his presence like he's physically touching me, and any thought I had of things being easier now that I know what it's like to *really* get close are swiftly gone from my mind.

If anything, it's harder to be around him now that I know what his touch feels like.

We're each other's dirty little secret and the thought of that excites me.

I have a part of him that no one else in this room does.

Maddy is talking again, going on about something Trevor did that pissed her off, and I find myself nodding at what I hope is all the right times, even though I have no idea what's really going on.

I can't think about anything other than Liam's lips on mine, his hands on my skin and the feel of his body against mine.

I don't know what's happening to me. I'm completely consumed by him.

I had a boyfriend for most of last year, and it was *nothing* like this.

I wasn't infatuated with him in this way. In fact, right now, as I look at Liam, I can't even remember my ex's name.

"Giiiirrl, you're crushing so hard on professor hotty."

A nervous giggle escapes from my lips as I drag my eyes back to my best friend.

"Shhhh," I hiss.

"Well did you get eyes for Christmas or something? Jeeze. I'm embarrassed for you," she teases.

I shake my head, trying to play off my nervousness as amusement. "Can you blame me?"

I figure at this point I'm better off to roll with it. Maddy can think I've got a harmless crush all she likes, as long as she doesn't know the truth, we're all good.

"Mmmm mmmm." She licks her lips. "No, I can*not*."

I pop a shoulder. "Exactly."

"So have you two got another date coming up or what?"

"Mads," I hiss at her, "Stop calling tutoring a date, before I slap you."

"*Periwinkle*," she raises her brows and gives me a 'you know I'm right' look, "you're so hot for that man you're almost bursting into flames. At least pretend you're dating him so I can live vicariously through you."

"You're insane." I groan. "And don't call me that."

"Periwinkle?" a deep voice says behind me, and I curse the day I ever met Madeline Dean.

"Li— Mr. Conrad, pretend you didn't hear that," I beg as I swivel around to face him.

"No can do." He grins, and I feel my cheeks blush bright red.

"*Please*," I beg again.

"I'll consider it... *Periwinkle*." He chuckles as he strolls down towards the back of the studio.

I blush deeper knowing that he not only just called me that, but he heard every word Maddy said about how hot I am for him.

"Well he's in a good mood today," Maddy whispers.

I nod my head in agreement.

I still can't believe that his mood might have something to do with me.

***

Half the class has filed out already, but I'm in no rush. I've got nowhere important to be until six o'clock tonight.

"You wanna get out of here?" Maddy asks, and I see that she's all packed up and ready to leave on time for once.

"Yeah, sorry, I was daydreaming."

"Oh, I bet you were." She smirks.

I hurriedly stuff my laptop into its case and into my bag before she picks up on the fact that I'm being slow on purpose.

I don't want to go anywhere, but I also don't want to draw unwanted attention.

I'm standing up when I hear him say my name. "Perry, before you go…"

Just the sound of my name in his sexy voice drives me crazy.

"Yeah, Mr. Conrad?"

"Can I see you for a few minutes, I wanted to show you something I thought could help with your project."

"Cha-ching, baby, date number two," Maddy says in a hushed tone as she brushes past me. "I'll see you at home, girl."

I wave out to her awkwardly and within a minute, we're the only two in the room.

Liam appraises me from head to toe, slowly, setting me on fire with just a glance.

"Do you know how hard it was to look at you this past hour and know I couldn't lay a finger on you?"

"I think I might."

I shift my weight from one foot to the other, not because I'm insecure, in fact when he looks at me like that, I'm anything but – I feel like the most beautiful woman in the world, but because I need to do something, *anything*, to stop myself from crossing the short distance between us and pressing my lips against his.

He must feel it too because, without warning, he strides to the door of the studio and shuts it firmly, locking it behind him.

He's back in front of me, gripping my hips and lifting me onto the work bench before I can even take another breath.

He settles between my legs, and I sigh in relief.

This is what I've been missing the past couple of days.

The feel of his hands on me.

"We shouldn't be doing this here, but I can't wait any longer," he growls as he places a soft kiss to my mouth. "You drive me *crazy*, Perry, I lose all self-control, all sense of reason when you're around."

I rest my forehead against his. I know how he feels, because I feel the very same way.

I don't reply, not with words, instead I kiss him, our tongues meeting in a frenzy.

"Are you still coming over tonight?" he asks when we finally break apart.

"If you still want me to?"

"You're a smart girl, Perry, I think you know the answer to that."

That makes me smile.

"What should I bring?" I ask as he rubs his nose against mine.

"Just your pretty face," he breathes. "I'll take care of the rest."

"You're sure? I can cook something, or pick something up..."

"Perry," he interrupts me, "let me take care of you."

I like the sound of that.

I've gotten so used to taking care of myself these past couple of years that I've forgotten how to let someone else do the job.

"Alright, click," I whisper, but the words get lost as he kisses me senseless all over again.

CHAPTER NINE

Liam

It seems like forever since I've cooked a meal for someone.

Perry should be here any minute; she text to let me know she'd escaped her housemates without too much of an interrogation.

I pace the room again, checking that the volume is up on the intercom so I know I'll hear her when she buzzes to come up.

I only live a few blocks from her, but our living conditions are slightly different.

She lives in a shitty student flat, and I... *don't*.

When I sold the house six months ago to move here, I thought I'd buy something else similar, but instead I found myself looking through this flashy apartment and deciding that it was a good fit for the new me.

I wanted a change and I got it.

I'm still not used to not having a lawn to mow, or a garden to weed, but for the most part, I like it here.

I go and check the oven for the five hundredth time. I'm shutting the door when I hear the intercom buzz.

I jog over and press the button. "Perry?"

I'm surprised by how nervous I feel.

"Hey," she replies, and I can hear the smile in her voice.

"Come on up." I press the release button, so she'll be able to get through the front door.

I jog to my door and fling it open hurriedly.

I seriously need to chill out. I take a deep breath and walk down the hallway towards the elevators.

I can't believe I'm *this* guy right now, the one betraying the trust of the university and my colleagues, not to mention everyone else in my life, but I'm not in control anymore. Not when it comes to her.

We're both adults. We're both willing, and we both want this.

I don't see how it can be wrong.

Except it is.

I know that. She knows that.

But neither one of us cares enough to stop it.

The elevator dings, the doors slide open, and just like that, all the guilt and any doubt falls away.

She's wearing a fitting, long sleeved, red dress and she's the definition of sexy.

"Wow." The one simple word falls from my lips, but it's not simple at all.

It carries so much weight, so much longing.

I wait for it, that blush that seems to be ever present when we're together, and it comes, right on cue, her cheeks turning a soft pink.

She steps out of the elevator, and I have to catch myself. I can't believe she's here to see me.

"You look amazing. How'd I get so lucky?"

I take her hand in mine and kiss her cheek.

"Stop, you're making me blush."

"I like that blush. Almost as much as those freckles." I tap the end of her nose.

She nibbles on her bottom lip, and I can't take my eyes off it.

I know I'm staring, but I can't help it.

A soft laugh falls from her lips. And I realise I'm standing here like an idiot.

"We should go inside before I burn the place down."

"That's reassuring," she teases as she lets me lead her down the hall to my apartment.

I chuckle. "It's been a while since I've cooked for anyone but myself, so if it tastes like shit, you'll know why."

She giggles as she steps into my apartment and I shut the door behind her. "You didn't bring a coat." I frown at her.

It's freezing out there.

She raises a brow. "Well I was trying to make a statement with the dress."

I take her in again. "Mission accomplished," I mutter.

She grins wickedly.

I don't want to rush things with her, but I'm not sure I'll be able to keep my hands off her when she's looking like that.

I gesture for her to follow me into the kitchen before I do something that will result in us winding up in my bed.

"This is a really nice place."

"Thanks, I'm still not sure I'm an apartment kinda guy, but it works."

"I'll trade you for my flat if you like?" She smirks.

I chuckle. "I did my time in shitty student flats, so thanks but no thanks."

"You said you went to uni here, right?"

I nod. "Sat in the same class I teach in now. I lived a few blocks away in quite possibly the crappiest flat in town – I actually think they pulled it down after we left. We cut a hole in the living room floor to throw the empty beer bottles into, and we had live bands play in the backyard nearly every weekend."

"A hole for empties?" She giggles. "That's next level dedication. I bet that draft was fun in winter."

"Scarred me for life." I chuckle. "Why do you think I've been chasing the sun for so long?"

I'd still be somewhere warm right now if I had my way, but instead I'm here. Not that I can bring myself to regret it, not right now with her next to me.

If she notices my moment of internal debate, she doesn't say anything.

"Smells good." She points to the oven.

"It looks edible enough."

"Don't go all modest on me now."

"Wouldn't dream of it." I chuckle as I check the settings on the oven yet again.

That's about all I can do. I just have to let it do its thing, and somehow try to act cool about having this beautiful woman in my home.

I stroll towards her and watch her as she watches me, her throat moving with a slow swallow.

She's so fucking drop dead gorgeous.

I can't get over it.

I bet she has men chasing her non-stop. Probably every one of those guys in my class has thought about asking her out at one point or another, but she's not off running around town with some college kid, she's here with me.

I stop in front of her, and she backs up a step until her ass hits the bench.

She looks up at me with wide eyes as I close the small gap between us, my arm coming around her back.

"You look incredible," I growl.

"I think you already told me that," she breathes.

I lean in, the stubble on my chin grazing her jawline as I breathe in the alluring scent of her.

Her arms reach up and wind around my neck, tugging me closer.

"It doesn't feel like enough," I murmur. "Incredible doesn't even come close to you."

"Liam," she whispers against my ear, and I lose it.

I lift her ass onto the bench in one movement and slide her legs open wide until I'm snugly between them, her dress riding up her thighs.

Her mouth comes down on mine in the same second, and we tangle together in a flurry of lips, tongues and teeth.

It's messy and rushed, but it's the hottest moment of my life.

I want her so badly I can't even remember my own name.

"Fuck, Perry," I growl as she kisses along my neck, down to my throat.

I've never wanted anyone this badly in my twenty-nine years, and I don't like the way I'm not in control of my emotions anymore.

I'm not in control of *anything* when it comes to her.

She could say jump, and I'd be right there asking how high.

Her hands slide around to my chest, her fingers gently playing with the buttons on the front of my shirt.

She slowly, deliberately, undoes the first one, before looking up at me for approval.

I don't know what look I'm giving her, but she drops her hands lower and undoes a second one, then a third until they're all undone, and my shirt is hanging loose in the front.

Her palms press against my bare skin, and a shiver runs down my spine.

"I wish I had my camera," she murmurs as her soft fingers explore every inch of my chest and stomach. "I've never seen something I wanted to photograph more."

"Me?"

"You." She nods, her hand stilling on my chest.

I don't know what to say to that. I've always been behind the camera; I've never considered myself worthy of being in front of it.

"Your heart is beating like crazy," she says softly.

"It's because of *you*."

"Me?" She bites down on her bottom lip, a shy smile tugging at the corners of her lips, and it cuts me like broken glass, right down deep inside of me, making its mark and leaving a scar that will never disappear.

I nod. "No one has ever made me feel the way you do."

Her eyes widen, her pupils dilating as she looks right at me.

She slips her hands up to my shoulders and down my arms, ridding me of my shirt.

It falls to the ground behind me.

The look in her eyes is pure want, and I know I'm not going to be able to resist her long.

"I wanted to take things slow with you," I say as her fingernails lightly graze the skin on my back.

"What if I don't like slow?" she purrs.

Jesus. She isn't making this easy. Actually, scratch that, she's making it entirely *too* easy to forget about being a gentleman.

"I can't get this wrong with you." I groan as she hooks her legs around my waist.

My hands are roaming her back and tugging through her hair, and I don't know why I'm arguing with her, this is everything I've imagined since I first laid eyes on her.

"Does this feel wrong to you?"

"*Nothing* about you feels wrong," I reply, my voice deep and gravelly with desire. "But I want you to know everything about me, I want to know everything about you before you give yourself to me."

Her fingers weave into my hair, our heavy breaths mingling in the small space between us as she mulls over my words.

"Alright." She sighs in defeat. "You're the most incredible man I've ever met, you know that?"

I chuckle. "Maybe I'm an idiot, I've got a beautiful woman right here in front of me, and I'm turning her down."

She smiles up at me, a sweet, sure smile. "I'm not going anywhere, click."

"Neither am I, freckles."

"Freckles?"

"I thought you'd like it better than Periwinkle." I chuckle.

She raises a brow but doesn't argue as I claim her lips with mine.

CHAPTER TEN

Perry

I blink my eyes sleepily as I'm pulled from my drowsy state by Liam's fingers trailing lightly up and down my thigh.

I can feel his firm, warm body behind me, and I realise that I'm lying on his couch and I've fallen asleep.

I glance at the TV, the movie we started watching is still playing, but it looks like it's nearly finished.

I twist around so I'm on my back. He's on his side, his front has been pressed against my back and his head is propped up on his elbow so he can see the screen over my head.

Only he's not looking at the screen, he's looking at me.

"You're back," he says softly as he reaches up to brush a few stray strands of hair from my face.

It's the sweetest thing, the way he does that. It's so tender and gentle.

"You should have woken me sooner."

He shakes his head. "You looked too peaceful."

His eyes hold mine, and I can see the total and utter sincerity in them. He could tell me the world was flat right now, and I'd believe him.

"I hope you don't mind me getting so close."

If I had my way, we'd have already got a hell of a lot closer before we even had dinner.

But no, he had to go and be all sweet and gentlemanlike and melt my heart to a puddle on the floor.

He might be the bad-boy teacher right now, breaking the rules by getting involved with a student, but that's not the real him.

The real him is genuine and honest, kind and considerate.

I learnt a lot about the real him over the course of the evening, so maybe he was right to want to take things slow.

If we'd ended up in bed, I wouldn't have found out that he has one older sister who is off travelling the globe, or that his dad passed away a while back, or that his mum lives with his aunt on the other side of the country.

I wouldn't have learnt that he can't stand photographing children but would take photos of animals any day of the week.

I wouldn't have learnt that his favourite place in the whole world is a small island off the coast of Greece, or that he is a fantastic cook.

I wouldn't have heard his stories about his wild uni days, or how he broke his arm when he was ten.

He wouldn't know any of those kinds of things about me either.

I know a lot more now than I did a few hours ago.

The most important thing I know now that I didn't then, is that I'm falling for Liam.

I know its crazy and stupid, but I'm doing it anyway.

He's watching me so closely, and I'm beginning to wonder if I'm one of those people who tells a story with their expressions, because when my name falls from his lips, it's a plea.

The hand that was stroking my thigh before resumes the action, only this time it goes higher and higher, sliding my dress up as it does.

He's ready now. He's wants this as much as I do.

I know I was the one pushing for this to happen earlier, but all of a sudden, I'm overcome with guilt.

He could lose his job for getting involved with me.

I know we've already crossed the line, but *this* is different. This can't be forgotten or brushed under the carpet the way a kiss could.

If we do this, cross this final line, we can never go back.

"Are you sure I'm worth it?" I whisper, my voice unsure.

"Worth what?" he murmurs as his hand finds its way to the bottom of my ass.

"Risking your career?"

His eyes soften. "You're worth risking *everything*."

Butterflies take flight in my stomach.

"Are you sure I'm worth risking *your* future?" he says as his lips kiss the skin on the underside of my jaw.

"Undoubtably," I breathe.

There's no question about it.

He chuckles and in a flash he's on top of me, his elbows supporting his weight as he presses me into the plush couch.

"I want it noted for the record that I tried to resist you, I really fucking did."

I giggle softly and push away the hair that has fallen into his eyes. "I might not know everything, Liam, but I know enough to want this with every part of me."

"That's good enough for me," he growls.

He pulls back, gets to his feet and holds out a hand to me.

I take it without hesitation, and he leads me past our disregarded movie, down the hall and into his bedroom.

He closes the door and looks back at me with a nervous expression.

"I haven't done this in a long time."

I reach for the buttons on his shirt for the second time tonight. I don't know if I believe that he hasn't had a woman in his bed lately, but I'm not about to question him about it. It's the last thing I want to think about.

I undo the last button and revel in the impressive sight in front of me.

I run my fingers from the waistband of his jeans, over his defined abdomen, all the way to his shoulders, and he physically shudders.

The simple gesture spurs him into action, and he spins me around, his nimble fingers finding the zip at the back of my neck and lowering it down to my ass in one fluid motion.

He slides the fabric slowly over my shoulders and down my arms, and now I'm the one trembling.

I can *feel* his eyes on my body.

I pull my arms free and he tugs the dress over my ass. It falls to the floor.

I expect him to turn me back around, but instead he appears in front of me, his fingers undoing his belt as he moves.

"Jesus Christ, Perry, do you know how long I've fantasised about that underwear?" His expression is almost pained.

It's the same set from Maddy's photography shoot, but I never expected him to notice.

"Do you like it?"

"Like it?" he growls. "Those pictures got me hard as a rock, and they've got *nothing* on the real thing."

My tongue darts out to moisten my lips, and he drops his head back with a groan.

"You're the most dangerous woman I've ever met."

I can't speak, I can't move, all I can do is watch.

He slides his belt out of the loops and tosses it onto the floor.

"I've imagined this moment for weeks."

He undoes the button on his jeans.

"I've dreamed about how I'd touch you, *kiss* you..."

He drags the zipper down painfully slow.

"I've fantasised about how it would feel to sink deep inside you."

"*Liam*," I beg, my voice hoarse.

I'm beyond worked up. His stare, his words, the way he's ever so slowly undressing himself is acting as foreplay for me.

He hasn't even touched me yet, and I'm on the verge of coming undone.

"Fuck, you're so beautiful." He huffs out a breath as his eyes travel over my body.

I feel beautiful when he's looking at me like that.

He circles me slowly, his hand gently caressing my ass as he moves, "I forgot to answer your question," he growls as he lingers behind me, his hands cupping my ass now.

"What question?" I breathe.

"The one about me being an ass or a tits man?"

"You heard that?" I blush.

He chuckles.

"So, which is it then?" I whisper.

"Ass," he says simply as he continues his trip around my barely covered body. "Definitely ass."

"Mmmm," I hum as his fingers skim up my side to my bra.

"Not that there's anything to complain about here either."

I can't take it any longer, the distance between us.

I throw myself at him, and he catches me against his bare chest.

He tugs the ends of my hair, and my chin tips upwards.

He doesn't say another word, just kisses me senseless as he backs me up to his bed.

His hands move to my shoulders and he pushes me backwards so I fall onto the covers.

He smirks at my surprised expression as he slides his jeans down, his hard dick springing free.

Well *damn*, professor hotty isn't wearing underwear.

"As much as I love that underwear, freckles, it's got to go."

I arch my back and reach behind me so I can undo the clasp on the sexy, lacy bra I'm wearing.

I hear his sharp intake of breath as I disregard it, but I don't stop, I reach for my underwear and slide them down my legs.

A primal, greedy noise rips from his throat before he's there on top of me, his hard length pressing against my thigh.

Neither of us say a word as he lines up to push inside of me.

He looks right into my eyes as he fills me, stretching me in the most delicious way.

"Jesus," he groans as his forehead falls to mine.

"Don't stop," I plead.

I thrust my hips upwards and he pushes back, taking me with a pace that has my eyes rolling back in my head.

CHAPTER ELEVEN

Liam

"Stop." She giggles. "We're going to get caught if we keep doing this here."

"Maybe I don't care," I growl as I continue kissing her neck.

"You do so," she says, her voice coming out like a moan.

"Who needs a job anyway?"

She giggles again and shoves me away. "Um *you* do."

I chuckle.

We've been all over each other this past week.

She's been at my place more than she's been at her own, and it's still not enough.

Now that I've had a taste, I want the whole thing, every second of the day.

I can't get enough.

I'm completely addicted.

The old me never would have pushed the boundaries like this in the first place, let alone so blatantly like I am right now, making out like a teenager in the storage room of my classroom.

"We better get out there before people start showing up."

I know she's probably right, but I don't give a fuck about the other students in my class right now, I only care about her.

She straightens her jacket and smooths down her hair and grabs a pack of paper from the shelf.

I look at her in question.

"That's what I came in here for." She smirks.

"Are you sure about that?"

"Yes, Mr. Conrad, I *am*."

I reach out to grab her, but she darts out of the way and bolts out the door and back into the studio.

I run a hand through my hair and chuckle.

It's not really funny, the predicament I've found myself in, and the situation is far more complicated than she realises, but I'm not ready to tell her about that, not yet.

I want to, I really do – I want to tell her everything, but I don't want to burst this bubble of happiness I've found myself in.

I never thought I'd feel this content again, and I can't risk ruining it yet.

I hear a voice outside the door, and I strain my ears to hear who it is.

I glance at my watch; I still have at least fifteen minutes before I'd expect any students to be arriving.

"You're in early," the voice says.

I hear Perry reply, "The early bird gets the worm, Mr. Radcliff."

"Shit," I mutter under my breath.

It had to be my best mate. The most perceptive bastard in town.

If anyone is going to notice that something is up, it's him.

I've brushed off plans with him twice this week already, and it's only a matter of time before he notices that the only student I ever seem to be alone with is the beautiful woman out there right now.

"Yeah, he's in the storage room I think," I hear Perry say, and I mumble a string of curse words as I work to do up the buttons on my shirt and wipe my mouth to make sure there's no sign of her lips.

I turn my back on the door and busy myself with a box of old negatives I found in here the other week.

"Hey, bro."

I turn around and hope that I look genuinely surprised. "Oh hey, Linc, what's up?"

"Just checking in," he says, as he leans against the door frame. "Haven't seen you for a while, thought something might be up."

I shake my head and go back to my fake sorting so I don't have to meet his eyes. "Nah I've just been busy, that's all. A few of the students have needed extra help with their work."

He's silent for a few beats, and I pretend not to notice how awkward it is.

"Her name's Perry, right?"

My pulse goes crazy. He's onto me.

"Huh?" I feign confusion.

He doesn't reply, and I glance back at him.

He tips his head in the direction of the classroom. "The hot one out there, her name's Perry?"

"Ah yeah... Perry." I make a show of glancing at my watch. "She's early."

I hope to god that my bullshit lie sounds more believable to him than it does to me, because to my ears, it sounds like a crock of shit.

"She seems to spend a lot of time here."

I shrug and turn away again. "She's a dedicated student, and no I'm not swapping for your uninterested jocks." I attempt a joke, but it falls flat.

He knows something is up with me, and I'm going to have to be a hell of a lot more careful than I've been being.

"Nicky told me to ask you over for dinner tomorrow night."

Nicky is Linc's wife. She's the sweetest little thing. They met here at uni; we all did.

"Tell her I'll be there; it'll be good to have a proper catch up with you both."

Hopefully that will get him off my back, because if he keeps up this interrogation, I'm bound to crack, and I *can't* crack.

I can't risk what Perry and I have.

"Alright, I'll tell her six o'clock?"

I give up messing around with the box of negatives and glance at my watch again, it's nearly time for class.

I nod. "I'll bring beer," I tell him with a grin.

He cracks a smile, but it doesn't quite reach his eyes.

He's still suspicious.

I take a step towards the door. "I better get out there."

He nods and steps out of the way so I can go past.

I feel my phone vibrate in my pocket, but I ignore it like I have been all morning.

I already know exactly who it'll be, calling *again*.

She's always ringing for something, and ninety percent of the time, I don't want to hear it.

Linc lingers in the room, his gaze drifting between me and Perry, who is dutifully ignoring him and working away on her laptop.

She's a hell of a lot better actor than I am.

"I'll see you tomorrow," he says, and I nod.

He casts one more glance at the woman who is starting to mean everything to me before leaving the room.

I release a deep breath and hear her giggle.

"I *told you* we were going to get caught."

"Yeah, yeah... no more storage room antics," I grumble.

She rolls her eyes, and I can't help but smile, even given the pressure I'm feeling.

Everything is all fucked up, but I think as long as I've got her on my side, I might just get through it.

***

It's a normal class.

Everything is going fine.

My phone has been vibrating non-stop in my pocket, and I've been cursing Lucia's name every few seconds, but other than that, it's business as usual.

Perry has been sneaking glances at me every so often, and I've been pretending not to notice, even though I know the small twitch of my lips gives me away.

I'm just about to sit down and plan out an online assignment when I hear footsteps running down the hallway towards the studio.

I'm on my feet, ready to meet whoever it is in a flash.

Half of the class turns as Linc bursts through the door, his face void of all colour.

"Linc, you okay?"

He shakes his head, and I feel my heart sink into my stomach.

My eyes dart to Perry in a panic.

He must know.

He knows I'm sleeping with my student.

"Shit, sorry, I need you to come with me," he says in a rush.

"I'm in the middle of a class, can't it wait until –"

"It *can't* wait," he interrupts me. "It's your wife, Liam, you need to come *now*."

My stomach sinks and I feel my own face pale.

I instantly feel guilty for ignoring my phone all morning, but that guilt is *nothing* compared to what I feel for what I've just done to Perry.

I can feel her eyes boring holes into my face, and I'm scared to look.

I don't know if I can handle the expression on her face right now, because I know it's bound to be a painful one.

I nod my head and turn to my class, being careful to avoid the front row with my eyes. "I'm sorry, I have to step out, please continue with independent study, and I'll see you next class."

I collect up my computer and my books and shove them into my bag as fast as I can make my hands move.

I can still feel her staring at me, and I know I can't walk out of this room without acknowledging her. I might be a bastard right now, but I still have a conscience.

I leave it until the last possible second and I'm glad I did because the heartbreak in her beautiful brown eyes almost brings me to my knees.

I'd give just about *anything* to be able to stop right now, to pull her into my arms and apologise profusely for what I've done, but I can't do that. Not here, not now.

I have to go.

I shoot her an apologetic glance and rush from the room.

CHAPTER TWELVE

Perry

Suddenly, fooling around with my teacher is the least of my worries.

Getting involved with a married man is.

The look he gave me as he rushed from the room was filled with guilt and sorrow.

I don't know if he's sorry because he got caught, or because he truly didn't want to hurt me, but I certainly know why he's guilty.

He's married.

It doesn't matter what that look meant when it comes down to it, because he *has* hurt me, crushed me even, and it's so painful I can barely breathe.

I try to suck in a deep breath but fail. I can't seem to get enough air to fill my lungs.

I've been sleeping with a married man.

I've been giving my heart to a man who has already given his to someone else.

I really am his dirty little secret, but not in the way I thought I was.

I gasp, trying to breathe again, and I hope that no one comes into the bathroom that I've rushed off to hide in.

I can't believe this is happening to me.

I'm totally floored by this revelation.

I thought we had something. Sure, it might have started out purely physical, but it's not felt like that this past week.

It felt like he was sharing every last piece of his soul with me, but I couldn't have been more wrong.

He was only sharing what he wanted to share, and I was too stupid to see it for what it was.

I think about his other students, his other classes and wonder idly if I'm the only one.

If he's willing to betray his wife in this way, why stop with one affair? Why not two? Or three? For all I know, he could have a girl in every class that he's messing around with.

My brain tries to repel the idea, everything I think I know about Liam tells me that it's wrong, that he *wouldn't* do that – that he's not that kind of guy, but *I'm* wrong, I remind myself.

The Liam I thought I knew isn't real. It was all a lie. An act.

He has a wife.

I feel dizzy as the word rolls through my brain yet again.

Wife.

I feel physically ill.

I rush from the sinks into one of the stalls, retching, but nothing is coming up.

I'm a homewrecker.

That's what his wife will call me when she finds out.

He could have children, a whole family at home.

I retch again.

I hear the door open to the bathroom, and I try to stop the sick feeling swirling in my stomach.

"P, you in here?"

I don't answer, but a sob rips up my throat that she's bound to hear.

"Are you crying? I know it's sad that professor hotty is married and all but *damn*," she jokes, but this is no joke to me.

This is very much a reality.

She knocks on the stall door, but I don't open it.

"C'mon, periwinkle, are you all good in there?"

"No," I reply, my voice cracking.

She knocks again. "Let me in or I'm climbing over the top." Her voice is serious now, there's no hint of joking.

I may as well let her in.

Knowing her, she really would climb in if that's what it took.

I slowly reach for the lock and flick it.

She's going to see me losing my shit, but I can't keep this to myself any longer.

I'm having a full-blown panic attack. I have to tell someone about this before I explode.

"Jesus, P, what the hell is wrong with you?" she demands as she sees the mess I am.

I gasp for another breath and slide to the ground, my back resting against the dirty bathroom wall.

"He's... he's *married*," I choke out.

"Oh sweetie, I know you had a crush, but this is kinda next level," she says as she crouches down in front of me. "You're being a little extra."

I shake my head. "You... you... you don't get it."

"I don't get *what*?" She frowns at me in confusion.

I breathe rapidly for a minute in an attempt to settle my pounding heart.

"Me and Liam..."

"What about you and Liam?"

I know I shouldn't be telling her this, Liam trusted me to keep it a secret, but I trusted him to be honest with me, and he clearly hasn't done that.

"We've been sleeping together," I whisper.

I watch as her eyes slowly widen, and her brows rise in surprise.

"You and professor hotty?"

I nod.

"Oh. My. God."

"He's married, Madds, I swear I didn't know."

I can feel tears rolling down my cheeks now.

I can finally breathe again, but now I'm bawling.

"Oh, Perry." She sighs as she pulls me in for a hug.

I cry against her shoulder, the sobs wracking through my body.

I can't believe I was so stupid.

She holds me for what feels like forever, until I'm not trembling anymore and I've run out of tears.

"Wait here, okay?" she says as she lets me go and passes me a handful of toilet paper to wipe my nose. "I'll go get our stuff and we're getting out of here. I'm taking you home."

I nod, numbness settling over me.

She gets to her feet and pulls the stall door closed behind her.

I hear her leave the bathroom, and I sit and wait, counting the seconds until she comes back.

***

"Here you go," Maddy says softly as she passes me a steaming cup of hot chocolate.

I'm curled up on the couch with a blanket and a box of tissues, even though I'm confident I'm all cried out.

I smile gratefully and take it from her.

I don't know what's wrong with me.

You'd think *I* was the one who just found out my husband cheated on me, not that I was the other woman.

I'm devastated, honest to god crushed from the inside out.

I've never felt this betrayed.

I didn't realise just how strong my feelings for Liam were until they were ripped out from underneath me.

Maddy sits down on the couch next to me and tugs some of my blanket over her legs.

"I know you're hurting, P, but I'm going to need you to tell me what the hell is going on here."

I knew she'd have questions. If there is one thing in the world that Maddy is thorough with, it's asking questions.

I nod. "You have to promise me that this stays between us, Madds, he could lose his job, and I could get kicked out of the course."

"Maybe I want him to get fired," she grumbles.

"*Maddy*," I warn.

She holds her hands up in surrender. "Fine, my lips are sealed."

I sigh. I don't know where to start.

I still can't wrap my head around the events that followed that stolen glance in the coffee shop on the first day of the semester.

We've had a connection ever since that first moment.

"I caught him staring at me in the café around the corner," I say when I figure out how to speak again. "I've never seen a man that looked like that."

She nods her head. "He is certainly something to look at."

"It wasn't until I got to class that day that I realised who he was."

"So you've been together all along? This whole time?"

I shake my head. "*No*... nothing happened until he invited me to go and take photos with him last weekend."

"*What*? Why didn't I know about this?" she demands dramatically.

I grimace. "Because I lied to you... well *technically* I didn't lie to you, I just didn't tell you the whole truth."

"You sneaky little bitch." She shakes her head in disbelief, but honestly, she seems a little proud.

"We went out to Rocky Hill – that's where he kissed me for the first time. It was perfect, the sun was rising and it felt like we were the only two people in the whole world."

"Wow."

I nod and smile sadly.

I'm reminded then of my dream of his wife catching us out there. It wasn't far off the money after all.

"So then what happened?"

I shrug. "Stolen kisses and looks... until I went to his house for dinner the other night when I told you I had a date."

"The deception just keeps on coming."

"Sorry." I wince. As painful as this is, it feels so good to get it off my chest. "Technically I *was* going on a date, just not with Brett from design class."

"What happened at his house...?"

I fiddle with the blanket on my lap. "He cooked me dinner, we talked, watched a movie... and then we slept together."

She looks so excited, I almost feel the need to burst her bubble and remind her that he's married, since she seems to have forgotten that small detail.

"It was good, right? God, I bet it was *incredible*."

"It was the best night of my life," I tell her honestly, fresh tears pooling in my eyes as I realise the truth in my words.

"I'm sorry, P, I shouldn't be asking you about him. You don't have to tell me anything else."

"I want to," I breathe. "It was starting to feel like it was all in my head, but it wasn't. It was real, Madds, the way he looked at me... I just can't believe it wasn't like that for him... he has a wife at home. How could he say those things to me, touch me the way he did when he's married to someone else?"

I'm staring at her, tears rolling down my face as I wait for her to answer me. I don't know what I expect from her, she hasn't got the answers any more than I do.

"I don't know, sweetie, I really don't."

I swipe angrily at the moisture in my eyes. I don't want to feel like this.

"He's really important to you, isn't he?"

I nod, my bottom lip trembling. "I thought I was important to him too."

She looks at me with so much sympathy. I break down again.

"There was no sign of a woman there, I swear I didn't know," I sob.

"Shhhh," she soothes. "Of course you didn't, I know you're not like that."

She's cradling me in her arms as I cry when I hear the front door open and Trevor call out, "Did you ditch class again you sexy bitch?"

I laugh, the sound muffled against her jersey.

"He's going to want to know what's going on," she says softly as she lets me go.

"You can tell him." I'd already accepted that by telling Maddy, I was telling Trevor too. The two of them have no secrets between them – something I'm seriously envious of right now given my current situation.

Trevor would never betray Maddy's trust – or mine, by telling anyone about this.

He strolls into the room and the devious smirk on his lips falls when he sees the state of me.

"P, what the fuck? Whose ass am I kicking?" he demands.

I giggle sadly, the laugh a gross, snotty mess.

"No one's, Trev, I'm okay."

"Like hell you are, you look like shit."

"Thanks," I mutter.

"Just give me a name, Perry, and I'll take care of it."

"You can't fix this one with your fists, trust me, babe," Maddy says.

Not if he wants to stay in university anyway.

They exchange a look that I don't understand, but Trevor stops making threats, so whatever it was, I'm grateful for it.

He strides forward, frowns as he looks at my tear-stained face and bloodshot eyes, leans forward to kiss my forehead and then stalks out of the room, muttering cuss words under his breath as he goes.

"He's a really great guy, Maddy, you did good with him."

"He is." She smiles fondly after him. "He cares about you, and he legit *will* want to kick some ass, but I'll talk him down. I promise."

"Thanks. Liam might have fucked me over but punching him isn't going to help anything."

"Madds!" Trevor bellows, his impatience obviously wearing thin. "Get in here."

"I better go and tell him what's going on before he breaks something."

I nod as she slides out from under the blanket.

"I'm really sorry, P, I know that doesn't help, but for what it's worth, I hope he feels awful about what he's done."

I don't reply.

God knows I feel awful enough for the both of us.

CHAPTER THIRTEEN

Liam

I escape to the safety of my car, start the engine and pull out onto the quiet, almost deserted street.

I only drive far enough to get out of sight of the house before I pull over again, I'm shaking so hard, I can barely keep the wheel straight.

I just had to get myself out of there.

I pull on the handbrake and let my head fall forward against the steering wheel.

Lucia was borderline hysterical as I drove away.

She was screaming and yelling, calling me names and throwing accusations around like venom.

I deserved it though.

I'm everything she accused me of being and worse.

The hardest part about it all was that the entire time she cussed me out, I wasn't thinking about the woman I should have felt guilty for betraying, I was thinking about the other one I've betrayed.

The one with dark hair and eyes, and a heart-stopping smile.

Perry.

I've fucked things up good and proper with her.

I can't even begin to fathom the hurt I've caused her in the hours since I walked out of that classroom.

I know I should steer clear of her, but I *can't.*

I have to see her.

I have to try.

I find myself releasing the handbrake and driving towards her flat, even though I know it's a stupid fucking idea.

She's not going to want to see me.

Why would she?

It's almost dark out, and I've got missed calls from Linc I need to return, but honestly, that's the least of my worries right now.

I've lied to every single person in my life this past month, but none I feel more guilty about than Perry.

She didn't deserve to find out like that.

I never should have lied to her in the first place.

I should have known that it wasn't going to end well... that she would find out eventually.

I must be operating on auto pilot, because it's as though I blink and then I'm coming to a stop outside her place.

My mind flashes back to the first time I came here to pick her up for our trip to Rocky Hill.

The day that everything changed between us. For better or for worse, it *changed*. My whole life was altered that day, that moment, the very second her lips touched mine.

I can't believe I've hurt her like this, because I *know* she'll be hurt – there's no way she couldn't be.

She's sweet, trusting and innocent in this whole mess.

She gave herself to me so willingly, and I took advantage of her. I'm undoubtably the one in the wrong here.

I kill the engine and sit in silence until I feel the cold creeping into my bones.

I can't put this off any longer.

I undo my belt, open my door and climb out of my car.

If I'm going to do this, I need to do it now.

I blow out a deep breath, and I see the steam in the freezing evening air.

I've got no idea what I'm going to say to her when I reach that door, but I know I have to say *something*. I have to try and make her understand.

I can't ignore this the way I've tried to ignore it in the past. I can't do it anymore, not to *her*.

I rap my knuckles against the wooden door and wait.

I know she lives with her friend Maddy and her boyfriend Trevor, so there's a good chance I'm going to raise suspicion by coming here at this time of the night, but I'm not even sure I care about my job anymore.

I don't know what I care about.

I just need to make things right with her. That's all I can think about now.

The door swings open and a tall, dark-haired guy stands in front of me. He's littered with tattoos and piercings, and honestly, I'm a little intimidated.

"*Well*, isn't this a surprise," he drawls. "To what do we owe the pleasure, *Mr. Conrad*?"

So, he knows who I am then, which means he probably knows *why* I'm here too.

"Trevor, right?" I question warily. I'm not here for a fight, and I have a feeling this kid would take great pleasure in trying to knock my head in.

He nods, his eyes hardening.

"Is Perry here?"

"Not if you're the one asking," he replies sharply.

Fuck.

He *definitely* knows.

"She told you?" I question, shame filling my voice.

He nods again. "She did, so if you know what's good for you, just leave and don't come back here again."

"I need to see her."

"You don't ne—"

"Trev, chill." Maddy appears from behind him, and I almost sigh in relief. Maddy knows me — I might have a shot of convincing her to let me in.

She steps in front of Trevor and crosses her arms firmly across her chest, her eyes narrowing at me.

"What do *you* want?"

"I need to see her, Maddy, to explain."

"What's there to explain? You're married."

"I know, but I need to talk to her. There are things I need to say."

"You really hurt her; you know that?"

I nod my head, my guilt overwhelming me. "I know."

I know and I hate it.

I'm not this guy.

I don't want to be this guy.

"Please," I beg, my voice broken, "I need to see her, just for a minute." I'm on the verge of tears, as pathetic as that makes me feel.

Maddy's eyes soften a fraction, but her staunch posture doesn't shift.

"It's okay, I'll talk to him," I hear Perry say, and I almost sag to the ground in relief.

Maddy glances back over her shoulder. "You sure, P?"

I don't hear what Perry replies, but whatever it is it convinces Maddy to move from her spot.

Her boyfriend, however, isn't so obliging. He stays put, shooting daggers at me.

"Trevor," Maddy snaps, tugging on his arm. "She'll be fine."

He growls something under his breath but steps back inside reluctantly. He shoots me a final warning glance. "You hurt her more than you already have, and I'll kill you."

I nod once in reply.

I don't know if I like this guy for being so protective of Perry or hate him for the same reason.

Whichever it is, it's all forgotten the moment she comes into view.

She looks truly exhausted, like she's been put through total hell and she's barely survived it.

She's been crying, not just crying, but *bawling* by the looks of things.

"Perry, I'm so sorry," I blurt out, and she looks like she's going to burst into tears all over again.

"What do you want, Liam?" she whispers, and the hurt in her voice crushes me, suffocates me from the inside out.

"I need to explain."

"Explain *what*?"

"About my wife."

She grips the door as the word finds her ears, her knuckles turning white.

"It's pretty simple really... are you, or are you not, married?"

"I am, but –"

"Then you need to go," she says as she closes the door in my face.

"Perry, *please*." I pound my fists against the door in desperation. "I can explain. It's not what you think."

The door flies open again, and this time she's not broken, she's mad – I've never seen Perry mad, and honestly, it's a little frightening.

"*Really*? *That* line? 'It's not what I think'? *How*? How is it not what I think, Liam?" she demands.

"She's my wife, okay, it's true, her name is April and she's my wife."

She opens her mouth to speak, but I cut her off. I need to get this out.

I can't recall ever having to say these words to anyone, but I'm going to now.

If I don't say this now, I never will.

"Nearly a year ago she was in a car crash. She suffered a lot of damage, to her body *and* her brain."

I hear her gasp.

I stare at my shoes as I spill my guts about the torment that has become my life.

"She's not the same woman anymore. She doesn't know me, Perry, my wife doesn't know who I am." My voice cracks.

"*Liam*," she whispers, her tone horrified.

I blink back the tears and carry on. "She lives with her parents now. I tried keeping her at our home with me for a while, but she was scared of me, I'm a stranger to her."

Perry slowly reaches for my hand, and I let her take it.

"Will she ever get better?"

I shake my head. "No. They say her brain is like that forever, she still looks mostly the same, but on the inside she's like a child. She's got the mentality of a seven-year-old. She'll never get better."

"Oh my god," she whispers, and I can't even look at her. "Today, why did you have to rush off? She didn't... she's okay, isn't she?"

"She's okay." I nod quickly. "She's got another lung infection. Her mum, Lucia, always flips out when something happens. She doesn't want my help unless something's going wrong. I try to move on with my life, and then she just drags me back in when it suits her."

I can feel tears spilling from my eyes now. I wipe them away angrily. I'm not the one with the right to be upset.

I shouldn't be here on her doorstep like this right now, after everything I've done. The last person who would be willing to comfort me is the woman in front of me.

"Liam," she says, and I finally find the courage to raise my eyes to hers.

There's no anger there anymore, no hurt, not even pity... there's just understanding and something else I can't place.

I swipe at a stray tear as it falls down my cheek, and she lunges forward, her arms wrapping around my waist in a vice-like grip.

I drop my head to her shoulder and hold her just as tightly back.

My tears escape silently, and honestly, it feels good to let out some of the emotions today has scarred me with.

"You should have just told me," she whispers. "I would have understood."

"I know," I murmur. "I should have, I'm so sorry."

"I'm so sorry you had to go through that."

"I could say the same thing to you. I'm so sorry about today, I can't even imagine how that felt."

"Forget it." She tugs away and forces me to meet her eyes. "But I need to know something, Liam,"

"*Anything*," I promise. I've got no more secrets, I'm an open book when it comes to her.

"Is there anyone else? Because I know we never talked about it, and we never agreed that we were exclusive..."

"There's only you, freckles," I answer quickly. "I know you probably won't believe me, but it's just you, you're the only one I see."

A small, shy smile graces her face, and I have to mentally pinch myself to see if this is real.

I never thought I'd get a chance to see that smile again.

"I believe you, but I don't know what to do anymore, Liam, I can't do casual, not with you, not after today." She shrugs, and I can hear the pain in her voice.

My heart swells in my chest, and I shake my head at her. "I don't want casual either. The past four hours – knowing how I'd hurt you – have been up there with the worst in my life, so that's how I know."

"Know what?" she asks hesitantly.

"That I'm in love with you. This isn't just fooling around for me, this is real. I love you, Perry, even if that means I've lost my mind."

She giggles, her eyes shining up at me with unshed tears.

"I'm out of my mind in love with you too."

CHAPTER FOURTEEN

Perry

I could have never predicated that things could turn out like this.

He's a broken man, I see it now.

There was sometimes an air of hesitancy about him, but I put it down to the unconventional nature of our relationship, when really it was so much more than that.

He's been harbouring demons I can't even begin to understand.

"Come inside, it's freezing out here."

He looks reluctant, probably due to Trevor and his threatening manner, but lets me lead him inside my house anyway.

I close the door and shut the chilly air out.

He shivers, like he didn't realise just how cold he was.

I lead him into the living room, and I only have to glance at Maddy and Trevor to know that they heard everything he's told me.

In a way I'm glad, it'll save me having to relay it to them.

I feel bad enough for them finding out about Liam and me, without having to share more secrets.

They get to their feet, and Maddy wipes a tear from her eye.

Liam glances awkwardly at them, and I'm about to try and clear the air when Trevor speaks. "We didn't mean to listen, but the walls are thin... I'm real sorry that happened to you, bro, that's a tough break."

Liam nods in appreciation. "Thanks, I uh...appreciate it."

"Mr. C, I really want to give you a hug, but I think we've all probably crossed enough lines tonight," Maddy says as she stands next to Trevor, rocking back and forth on her heels.

"I think that's probably right." Liam chuckles, but even through his smile, his exhaustion is obvious to me.

"I just wanted you to know that your secret is safe with us, we're not the kind of people to go ratting on our friends."

"Thank you," I reply. I know they're speaking to Liam and not me – I already know they'd *never* tell, but I also know he's worn out. I can see how tired he is.

I turn to him. "Can I come home with you, stay the night? I don't think either of us should be alone tonight."

He reaches out, his hand cupping my jaw. "That's the best idea I've heard all day."

***

We're tangled up in one another, the covers of his bed pulled up to our chins.

We haven't done more than kiss, but it's enough.

I just need to know he's here, and I think that's all he needs from me too. Comfort.

He's been all alone in a lot of ways, and I'm not sure that he's had anyone look after him in a long time.

I know Mr. Radcliff – *Linc*, has been really good to him, and Liam's sister has supported him a lot too, but she's over the other side of the world now, and Lincoln has a wife and baby at home to occupy his time.

Liam told me they all met at university. Linc was dating Nicky and Liam was dating April. April and Nicky became friends after the two guys introduced them, so this is bound to have been hard on them too.

Liam and April had been married for two years when the crash happened, Nicky and Lincoln were the only ones that were there to witness their marriage.

They've all been in each other's lives a long time.

It must be hard for Liam to see his best mate happy with his wife when his own isn't the woman he once knew.

"What was she like?" I whisper into the silent room.

There's no one here to overhear us, we don't have to sneak around, but I don't want to disturb the peacefulness of this moment.

His hand finds mine and he intertwines our fingers. He sighs heavily before answering me. "She was bright and bubbly and full of attitude. That much hasn't changed actually; she's still all of those things." He huffs out a laugh.

"That's something I guess, at least she didn't lose herself entirely."

"She hated pizza and snow. She loved cats and chocolate milkshakes."

I laugh lightly.

I feel him turn so he's facing me in the darkness.

"She was a good woman."

"You really loved her," I say, and there's not an ounce of jealously in my body. If anything, there's only sadness. It hurts me that he lost something he clearly treasured.

I can't imagine losing someone you loved that much.

If I were to lose Liam like that, it would *kill* me, and we're not even married, we certainly don't have nearly a decade of life together under our belts.

I can't even begin to fathom the hurt he suffered.

"I did. I still do, even though she's not the same anymore."

"She's lucky to have someone like you love her, click."

He chuckles softly at the nickname. "You think?"

"I know. I bet she loved you too."

He's quiet for so long I start to wonder if he's fallen asleep.

"Sometimes I wish she'd just died in that crash. I know it's a terrible thing to say, but she never would have wanted to live like this."

It sounds harsh, but I understand what he's saying; she isn't herself anymore, and he's had to mourn the life of someone who didn't die. It must be an impossible task.

"Is she happy at least?"

"Some of the time, I guess." He sighs. "She was in a coma for a long time, she got a lot of infections, and now her lungs aren't doing what they're meant to, among other things. She has a lot of health issues now."

"That's heart breaking."

I can feel the tears pooling in my eyes, and I'm grateful we're in the dark. The last thing I want is for him to feel like *he* needs to comfort *me*.

"It's horrific to watch. When she's good she wants to play barbies and paint her nails with glitter polish, which is just *wrong*... and when she's bad, she just cries and sleeps all the time, and when that happens, suddenly kids' toys and all things pink don't seem so bad after all."

I feel so awful for April, I really do, but it's April's parents who must be suffering the worst of all. Watching someone you love, someone with so much potential be reduced to that is truly torture.

His grip tightens on my hand.

"You know what I can't get my head around, though? The thing that's confusing me the most about everything?"

"What?" I whisper.

"That it was never like this with April. I fell for her slowly, we'd been in the same circle of friends for a year before we even went out on a date. I never really thought of her that way, but I grew into it I guess... but with you... it hit me like a freight train, Perry, one look at you and I was hooked."

I can't form words to reply to him.

"I *had* to have you, it was like I didn't have a choice... From that moment in the coffee shop I was yours and you were mine, even if you didn't know it."

"I felt it," I whisper. "It was like that for me too... the way it felt when you looked at me across that room, I can't explain it... maybe karma thought you were owed a break."

"Karma could have waited until the end of the year when you weren't my student anymore, if it *really* wanted to give me a break." I can hear the grin in his voice.

I muffle my laugh in the pillow. "Now you're pushing it."

I feel his fingers brush over my hair. "I don't care, you know that?"

"About what?"

"That I'm jeopardizing my career, that I'm breaking the rules... I don't care about any of it. Nothing should be worth this risk, but *you* are – you're the exception, and if that means we have to keep secrets and sneak around for another few months, then so be it – I'm all in."

I'm sure as hell in. Especially now that Maddy and Trevor know. It's easy for me. I barely have to hide this from anyone, but Liam *does*, and I hate that.

He has to keep secrets from his colleagues, his friends... everyone in his life except me.

"What about Linc?"

I feel him shrug. "I'll wait until you graduate and then we can tell him that we've just started dating."

"You think he's going to believe that?"

"I don't know..." He sighs. "I think he already suspects something is up, but like I said, I'm not sure I really care anymore. I can always find another job."

"You can't get fired because of me."

"I'd get fired for you in a heartbeat, freckles, as long as I knew you could graduate."

He really is the sweetest man. But he won't be getting sacked. Not on my watch.

He yawns, and I feel him settling deeper into his pillows, his body relaxing into sleep, but my mind is still ticking.

I'm curious about his wife.

"Liam?" I whisper.

"Yeah?" he replies sleepily.

"April... I want to meet her."

I don't know if he falls asleep, or he pretends not to hear me, but either way, I don't get an answer.

CHAPTER FIFTEEN

Liam

I grin at her as she bounces excitedly in her seat.

I reach over and run my hand over her jean-covered thigh.

She loves it when we get out of town.

We don't have to hide; we can walk down the street hand in hand and not one person bats an eyelid.

I think we've been to every little town within a two-hour radius these past couple of months.

As much as I hated Perry finding out about April the way she did, it actually worked out to be for the best. Maddy and Trevor being in on our little secret, and more than that, being cool with it, has made Perry's life so much easier.

She doesn't have to lie to her friends, and she can come over to my place whenever she wants, which is often.

More than often.

If we're not in classes, we're usually together, aside from the time I've been spending with Linc.

He's been less suspicious lately, and I'm grateful for it. I hate lying to him, but I have limited choices here, and not having Perry in my life simply isn't one of them.

My life hasn't felt this full since before the accident.

She looks at home in my living room, even if she's just working on an assignment, or watching basketball curled against my side. She's more comfortable in my kitchen than I am, and I swear to god she was made to sleep in my bed.

But even with all these tensions easing up, it's somehow getting harder, *impossible* even. I want to show the world that I'm with her – that this incredible woman is *mine*, and I can't.

It's harder to deal with than I could have ever imagined.

We just have to get through the rest of the year. She'll graduate, and I won't be her teacher anymore.

We'll be free.

"Where are we going?" she asks again, and I chuckle.

I'm not sure why she thinks I'm going to be anymore inclined to tell her now than I was half an hour ago, but god loves a trier, I guess.

"You'll see when we get there."

She scowls. "Can't you just give me one little hint?"

"Nope."

"You're no fun."

I think she'll be singing a different tune when she does find out where I'm taking her.

If there's two things I've learnt about Perry during our time together, it's that she loves antiques, and that she doesn't like me spoiling her.

So I figure if I'm going to go against her wishes and spoil her, then it has to be with something from an antique store.

I'm all about balance.

It took hours of online research to find this place, but I think she's going to love it, and that's all I care about.

It's been forever since I planned a real date, and it's taken me right back to my uni days.

Perry has that effect on me, and not just because she's close to ten years younger than me, but because she makes me feel like a teenager in love all over again.

I don't even notice our age gap anymore. She's not like any other twenty-year-old I've met; she's wise beyond her years, and talented beyond all expectations.

She's a model student – other than the fact she's having a secret affair with her lecturer – and she's just a beautiful person in general.

Everyone loves her. Me most of all.

She catches me looking at her and grins.

I know when I picked her up this morning, she thought we were going to finally go and see April together.

I don't know what's been holding me back, but there's something.

I guess I'm scared.

I'm scared to show Lucia that I've moved on. I'm afraid of Perry being scared off by the reality of seeing April in the flesh.

It's a lot for her to deal with.

Most of her friends are out drinking in the weekends, going to parties and hooking up with loads of guys, but not my Perry.

She cares more about me than any of that.

It hits me then, that *she* cares about *me* more than seemingly anything else.

I need to give her the chance to make up her own mind about the skeletons in my closet.

Suddenly I wish I *was* taking her over to visit the woman I married rather than to some small shop three hours from home.

We slow as we approach the 'Welcome to Sherrington' sign and Perry glances at me curiously.

"You ever been here?" I question.

She shakes her head as she presses her nose against the window to watch the tiny town slowly go by.

Nothing seems to have changed in this town in the past fifty years, it's like the whole place came to a standstill, and everything here just got frozen in time.

It's got charm, beauty and elegance, just like my girl.

"It's so cute," she breathes as I pull into a park and kill the engine.

She pulls her face from the glass and shifts around to look at me. "We're getting out here?"

I grin. "This is where the surprise is."

She shrieks in excitement and throws open her door.

I chuckle as I watch her rolling out her shoulders and smoothing down her jacket.

She must hear me laughing, because she turns back around, bends down and pokes her tongue out at me through the window.

Her nose and cheeks are already starting to turn pink from the chill in the air.

The snow will really settle in soon.

The thought of it on the roads makes me uneasy, it had nothing to do with the crash April had, but it causes so many more accidents on the roads around this part of the country, which just makes me nervous.

I'd hate to see what happened to April, happen to anyone else.

I unbuckle my belt and climb out to join her.

She reaches out for my hand, and I take it in mine, bringing it up to my lips to kiss it.

It makes her blush, and I love that I still have that effect on this confident, self-assured woman.

I swing our joined hands between us as I watch her take in the charm of this little town.

She wishes she brought her camera with her; I can see it in her eyes.

"Pretty as a picture, isn't it?"

She smiles up at me, and I swear my heart stops. I don't think I'll ever get used to that light in her eyes.

"You know me too well."

She starts to stroll towards the centre of town, and I tug her hand in the opposite direction.

I can see the antique shop's sign about half a block down.

She narrows her eyes at me, a smile tugging at the corners of her mouth.

She's one of those people who loves and hates surprises at the same time.

"C'mon, you'll love it."

We only walk another few metres when she spots it. "An antique shop?" she asks excitedly.

I nod. "I found it online. I thought you might want to pick something out for your birthday."

Her jaw falls slack, and I chuckle, a deep, throaty laugh. "That's right, freckles, I know it's your birthday next week."

"Did Maddy tell you? Because I told her not to." She pouts.

I shake my head. "You're forgetting I'm your teacher, baby, I have access to all your information."

"*Mr. Conrad*," she gasps in fake outrage, "you wouldn't be using school resources for personal gain now, would you?"

"You bet that sweet ass I am." I smirk as I hold the door open for her to enter the shop.

"Good morning, how are you both today?" the jolly-looking man behind the counter calls out to us as the little bell above the door notifies him of our presence.

This place is so old school, I'm actually starting to wonder if this is an antiques shop at all, or just a regular store around these parts.

"We're great thanks, how are you?" Perry responds brightly as her eyes sparkle.

"I'm very well, thank you, dear."

She's already looking at all the treasures this little place holds.

She loves all things old; she loves taking something from another era and making it at home in this one.

I chuckle and let go of her hand, shooing her off to go and look around.

I need to have a word with Marvin anyway.

Perry disappears further into the store and I hear 'oohs' and 'ahhs' along the way.

"Marvin, right?" I extend my hand to the silver-haired man.

"Are you the young gentleman I spoke to on the phone?"

"Liam." I nod. "And I sure am."

He smiles widely and peers around the store, but there's no sign of Perry – she could look around for hours. "Is she the lucky lady?"

"I could argue that I'm the lucky one, but it's for her... if she likes it, that is."

"She'll love it, I can already tell." He smiles warmly as he reaches under the counter and brings out a small wooden box.

I spent countless hours scouring online stores and emailing jewellery brokers until I found just the thing I was after.

It wasn't easy, but when I found out it was only a few hours' drive away, I figured it was meant to be.

He opens the box and reveals the antique oval locket. It's gold, with intricate designs etched into the metal, the chain is delicate and pretty – just like Perry.

"It's perfect," I murmur as I reach for it.

He removes it from its plush interior and hands it to me.

I gently open it and see that it has space for two photos. That's never going to be enough for a photographer, but it's better than nothing.

"What do you think?"

"I think she's going to love it." I smile at him.

I had intended to show it to Perry here, but now that I've seen it, I don't need to. It's everything I thought it would be and more.

"I think I'll keep it a surprise," I whisper, glancing around to make sure Perry is still immersed in the antiques.

He nods knowingly and takes it back from me, tucks it back into position and closes the lid.

I slide him the cash we agreed on and he passes me the box which I slip into my jacket pocket.

"Warms my heart to see romance alive and well." He beams, his voice hushed. "My wife will go all doe-eyed when I tell her about the two of you."

I don't know why, but it makes me blush.

I've never thought of myself as a romantic kind of guy, but after what I've been through with April, I've figured out a few things about life and about myself.

Mainly that it's short – too short not to let people know how you feel, too short not to treat those you love like they mean the world to you.

So, I'm going to show Perry just how important she is to me, every single day for as long as she'll let me.

"Oh my gosh, Liam, you have to see this."

I grin and Marvin gestures for me to go ahead.

I find her at the very back of the store, looking at an old, antique record player.

"My nana had one just like this when I was little," she coos, her eyes soft and warm as she looks at it. "We used to put a record on and dance to the songs. Mum always said that's where I got my love of the past from, after grandad died, nana simply refused to move ahead with the times... she had all kinds of old stuff."

That's either the sweetest thing I've ever heard or the saddest. Maybe both.

"We should get it."

She huffs out a laugh. "I don't know about you, but this doesn't exactly come within a student's budget."

She starts to move on, looking at other things, but I grab her hand and tug her back against my chest. "I'll get it for you."

She laughs again, but it dies off when she takes in the serious expression on my face. "Don't be silly, it costs a bomb."

I shrug. "So what?"

I glance at the price tag, it's not even that bad. If she knew what I just paid for the gold in my pocket, she'd have a heart attack.

"Liam, you are *not* buying that for me."

"Fine," I reply, and she breathes out a sigh of relief. "I'll buy it for *me*."

I let go of her hand and head back to the counter to tell Marvin that I'll take it, along with a collection of records.

She argues with me the entire time, in fact she's still arguing with me about it while I load it into the boot of the car. She argues while we get brunch, and for most of the drive home too.

She finally relents when it's set up in my living room, and I ask her to dance. That really gets her.

I smile down at her, my heart falling even deeper for her with every passing second. "This was a good choice." I point to the gold hair pin she eventually let me buy for her, under the pretence that it was an early birthday present.

"I love it, thank you, it's a beautiful gift."

It's not her only present, but I'll let her think it is, for now at least.

"So, I was thinking..." I say as I spin her out and back in.

"Sounds dangerous," she teases.

"I never gave you an answer about meeting April."

"You didn't."

"I was thinking I could take you over there tomorrow, if you still want to go, that is."

I shift nervously from one foot to the other, the dancing forgotten.

"Really?" she asks in a whisper.

I sweep her hair away and kiss her forehead. "If that's what you want?"

"I'd love to meet her, click."

"Well then it's settled, I'll let Lucia know we'll be over there tomorrow."

Perry looks so happy, but truthfully, I'm terrified. Introducing your girlfriend to your wife isn't exactly the norm, but I guess if this is going to last with Perry then I have to let her see everything, the good, the bad, the ugly... *everything*, and hope that she loves me enough to stick around once she's seen it all.

CHAPTER SIXTEEN

Perry

Liam is so nervous. I can tell by the way his eyes keep darting to mine, seeking me out for comfort, and the way his knee keeps bouncing up and down as he drives us over to April's parents' house.

I understand this must be strange for him.

It's strange for me too.

I never thought I'd be in my final year of university, dating one of my lecturers, head over heals in love and about to meet the woman he promised his life to.

He pulls into the driveway of a tidy-looking house, only a ten-minute drive from campus, and kills the engine.

"Do they know I'm coming?" I ask absently as I glance out the window.

"I told Lucia I was bringing a friend, but I haven't elaborated any further."

"You don't think she'll be happy for you?" I ask, sensing that that is the real reason he hasn't said anything, and also the reason it's taken this long for this meeting to happen.

I knew he wasn't ready, and I wasn't going to push it with him.

I knew he'd make it happen in his own time, but now that we're here and he still seems so unsure, I wonder if I have pressured him in some way.

"I'm honestly not sure, she kind of runs hot and cold when it comes to me, so I never really know what to expect when I walk in that door."

"If you're not ready, we can come back another time?" I offer.

He shakes his head and smiles the first genuine smile I've seen since we left his place. "I'm ready, freckles, I just hope you don't get scared off."

"*That's* what's got you sweating?" I gape at him. "You're worried I'll run?"

"Any sane person would," he mutters as he runs his hand through his hair. "It's a lot, Perry, a fucking lot of shit inside that house."

"I don't care. All I care about is *you*, and if that means seeing what you're dealing with, then that's just part of the package. I can handle it."

He studies me for a few beats, looking for any indication that I'm not being honest, but he won't find any. I mean what I said.

"You really are too good for me."

"Yeah, I know," I say, my tone teasing, "And I'm too young for you too, but do you think we should go inside now?"

I open the door and step out onto the driveway.

He chuckles and follows suit.

We walk towards the door, and just when I start to wonder what he's going to tell them about the status of our relationship, he reaches down and takes my hand in his.

I guess that answers that.

I squeeze it tightly as he knocks on the door.

I can hear talking and some shuffling around and when the door opens, it's a middle-aged woman who appears.

"Hey, Lucia, sorry we're late."

She gives Liam a tight smile and then her gaze drifts to his hand in mine before coming up to my face.

"And who is this?"

"This is Perry... my girlfriend."

Her eyes widen slightly in surprise, but she doesn't comment.

"It's nice to meet you, Lucia, I've heard a lot about you all."

"Well then... I've heard nothing about you," she says as she ushers us indoors.

"We've only been seeing each other a few months," Liam explains.

"I see," she replies, her lips pursed.

It's becoming clear that Liam was right to be wary of announcing he was in a new relationship.

"Frank," she calls down the hallway, "Liam and his friend are here."

I don't miss the way she calls me his 'friend' rather than his girlfriend like she's just been told I am.

I hear a grunt from the direction she just called out and then a guy who looks like he's in his mid-sixties wanders out.

"Hey, Frank, it's good to see you," Liam says, and the smile on his face is real this time, not fake like it was when Lucia opened the door.

"Liam," he replies cheerily, "did you see that game last night?"

"I did, they never looked like losing."

The two men shake hands and then he turns to me. "And who is this pretty young lady?"

"Young is right," Lucia mutters. No one else acknowledges her so I pretend I didn't hear her comment.

Frank reaches for my hand and clasps it in his.

"I'm Perry."

"Perry." He smiles. "It's good to meet you."

Liam clears his throat, "Is April awake? Perry would really like to meet her."

"She was awake early so she's probably sleeping, and I've actually got a few things I wouldn't mind going over with you in the kitchen." She points in the direction Frank came from.

"Oh leave it, Lucia, the boy doesn't need to worry about any of that. You two go on down to her room and see her, she'll be happy to have some visitors. She's been bored to death lately."

He gestures for us to go past them, and I can't help but wince at the death glare his wife is giving him, even though he seems totally oblivious.

Liam takes my hand in his again and tugs me past a seething Lucia, and a grinning Frank.

I know that woman hasn't had it easy lately, but she seems like a real piece of work.

"Sorry about her," Liam murmurs as we walk down the hallway.

I can hear music playing, pop music by the sounds.

"Sounds like she's awake after all," Liam muses.

I'm aware that Lucia is hot on our heels, and the humph noise she makes, lets me know she heard his comment.

Liam leads me into a room painted bright pink and covered in all sorts of bright pictures and posters.

He knocks gently on the door. "Hi, April."

She's sitting on the bed, cross-legged. She looks up at him but doesn't say anything.

She's beautiful. Totally and utterly drop-dead gorgeous... and she's sitting there with her hair in pigtails and wearing an Ariana Grande t-shirt.

"April, are you going to say hello to Liam?" Lucia asks her.

"Hello, Liam," she parrots, just like a child being prompted by their parent.

It's heart-breaking.

"It's good to see you, April... I brought someone to meet you today, is that okay?" Liam asks her.

He tugs me further into the room, and April looks at me. She smiles. I take that as my cue to speak.

"Hey, April, I'm Perry."

"You're *really* pretty."

Well that's not what I was expecting her to say.

"Um thanks, so are you."

"Do you want me to paint your nails?" she offers.

I look to Liam for help but he just shrugs, a bewildered expression on his face.

Lucia seems just as surprised by April's suggestion.

"I think purple would look good on Perry, do you have any purple, princess?" Frank asks from his spot in the doorway.

He gives me an encouraging nod.

"Sure do. Do you want purple, Perry?"

Why the hell not, it looks like I'm getting my nails painted.

"I like purple," I say as I cross the room and sit down on her bed.

I don't know what I'm meant to do here, but if letting her paint my nails keeps her happy then so be it.

She takes my hand in hers and lays it flat on her knee.

She grabs the bottle of bright purple polish from the huge basket of little bottles and twists the cap off.

"So, you like Ariana?" I ask.

She smiles and nods furiously. "She's my *favourite*. Mum said if I'm well enough, she'll take me to her concert when she comes to town next."

"That sounds like a lot of fun. I saw her once a few years ago, she was really good."

Her jaw drops. "I'm so jealous."

I smile sadly at her. She's got so much to be jealous for when it comes to me – I'm in love with her husband after all – but I don't know if it's a relief or a burden that her only concern is a pop singer.

I watch as she carefully swipes the polish over my nails, before tilting her head to the side and studying her handiwork.

I glance back towards the door and see that Lucia and Frank are gone.

Liam is still there though, leaning against the door, watching us with glistening eyes.

I can't imagine how hard this is for him.

"Are you okay?" I mouth the words across the room to him.

He nods quickly, a smile gracing his face, and his gorgeous dimple showing. "I love you so much," he mouths back.

My heart skips a beat.

"I think he likes you." April giggles, and I realise she's been watching our exchange.

"I think you might be right."

Liam watches us for a few more minutes, a wide grin on his face, before he disappears out the door.

April doesn't even notice.

"Done," she announces proudly as she puts the final layer on my thumbnail.

While she's worked, we've listened to her favourite Ariana Grande song three times and she's shown me a picture of Harry from One Direction that she thinks is 'totally cute' – her words, not mine.

I wave my nails in front of my face. She talked me into a glitter topcoat at the last minute, but I have to admit, they're actually pretty cute.

"Thank you so much, I love them."

"Really?" she asks hopefully.

"Really." I grin.

"Are you going to come visit me again?" she asks. "Liam comes sometimes, but he's not very fun to talk to."

"You should offer to paint his nails next time," I say with a grin.

She giggles.

"If you want me to come again, and it's okay with Liam, then I'd love to," I promise her.

"That would be cool."

She yawns a big sleepy yawn, and I'm reminded that she has a brain injury, and she might need to rest.

"I think it's time for us to go, but thanks again for the nails, and I'll see you next time, okay?"

She nods, and I can tell she's going to crash out the moment I leave.

I get up off the bed and make my way from the room.

She lays down on the pillows and I watch her for a moment.

I feel like crying.

She's so sweet and she seems happy enough, but it's devastating to see a person have their potential taken away like that.

As far as the doctors are concerned, she will stay in this mental state for the rest of her life – her short-term memory has been affected as much as her long-term.

I wander back down the hallway, pausing to look at the photos hanging on the walls.

There's one of Liam and April on their wedding day. They look so happy and in love; it hits me right like a punch to the gut.

He's lost so much.

April probably wouldn't even recognise that as herself.

"I don't know what you were thinking, bringing her here," I hear Lucia hiss.

"She's my girlfriend, she wanted to meet April. *Of course* I brought her here, she's a part of my life now," I hear Liam reply. His tone sounded pissed off.

I linger awkwardly in the hallway, I don't want to interrupt their conversation, but I also don't think I should stand out here eavesdropping like this.

"She's a little young to be taking too seriously, isn't she?" Lucia throws back at him.

"Lucia, that's not your business, she seems like a very nice young woman," Frank interjects.

"Not *my* business?" Lucia screeches.

I hope April is a deep sleeper, because her mother certainly isn't keeping her voice down.

"He's married to *my* daughter, for crying out loud, and I think it makes it my business when he starts parading some girl around my house."

"I wasn't parading her around, I was bringing her here to meet April," Liam says, and his tone sounds tired now, like he's lost all the fight in him.

I don't know why he's letting her talk to him like that.

"It's totally inappropriate, not to mention disrespectful. You're *married*, Liam, you shouldn't have a girlfriend in the first place," she scolds him.

"She's not his wife anymore, Lucia, we've been over this. She is not the woman he married. You need to let him live his life." Frank's voice is raised now, and I really want to go in there, but my feet are frozen to the ground.

I can hear Lucia sobbing now, but I'm not buying into her pity party.

The way she's talking to Liam is totally unfair. She's being outright nasty when she doesn't need to be.

I'm sure this is hard for her, but she can't expect Liam to spend the rest of his life committed to a woman who doesn't even say hi when he enters a room.

He's not even thirty yet. He's got a lot more life to live.

"Well it's *all* his fault," she screeches, and I flinch as though she's slapped me. "If it weren't for him, she'd be fine."

"I know you're upset, but that isn't fair, Lucia, you know it wasn't Liam's fault. It was an accident – what happened isn't *anyone's* fault." Frank's voice is soft, but firm – it's clear to me that this isn't the first time they've had this conversation – or screaming match, whatever you want to call it.

"I think I should go," I hear Liam say.

"No! We need to make some decisions about her medical treatment," Lucia starts again, her voice borderline hysterical. "You don't just get to swan off with your new woman like some playboy and leave us here to do all the work."

I see red.

A 'playboy' is the furthest thing from Liam.

He's sweet, kind and loyal.

From what I've just heard, that woman in there blames him for what happened to her daughter, and the last thing Liam needs is the weight of that on his shoulders.

I burst into the room, my breathing heavy.

Three heads snap around to look at me.

"Perry, how much of that did you hear?" Liam asks, his voice pained.

"Enough."

I open my mouth to let rip on his mother-in-law, but he rushes towards me and tows me from the room, out into the hall. His hands are shaking, and all I want to do is wrap him in my arms and never let go.

All my anger dissolves when I see the undeniable hurt in his eyes. He doesn't need me going off – there's already been enough yelling.

"You can't let her talk to you like that," I whisper.

My heart is beating so fast it feels like a blur. I hate that he's in pain.

"I don't know what else to do, freckles. She blames me, and maybe she's right."

I frown at him. I don't understand why anyone would blame him for a crash he wasn't part of. "It's not your –"

"April went out to get more beers for Linc and me – we ran out and she hadn't had a drop to drink. That's when she had the crash," he interrupts me.

That doesn't make it his fault. It was an *accident*.

Jesus Christ.

He's spent too much time in the room with that awful woman. He's starting to believe the horrible things she's filled his head with.

"This wasn't your fault. You know that, right?" I clasp his face in my hands and force him to look right at me. "You don't blame yourself for what happened, do you?"

He blows out a breath. "No. *Maybe...* I don't know. It's just easier if I'm her punching bag – she's mad at the world and she needs someone to take it out on. I figure it's the least I can do."

"You're hurting too," I say, my voice trembling with emotion. "You don't have to do this. She can find a new punching bag. You don't owe it to her, Liam – this isn't your burden to carry."

His head falls forward until his forehead is resting against mine, his arms wrapping tightly around my waist.

"You've got enough of your own hurt, click, don't drown yourself in hers too."

He nods but doesn't speak.

"I'm going to give you guys some space to talk," I whisper.

"Don't go, you don't have to go," he begs.

"I do," I reply firmly. "You need some time, and honestly, so do I."

"You're leaving?" he chokes out.

I bring my face up to meet his and kiss him softly on the lips. "I'll be at your place – whenever you're ready to come home, okay?"

He nods reluctantly, and I pry myself free of his grip.

I slip out the door without looking back – I can't stand seeing the hurt in his eyes – and begin the walk back to his apartment building.

I've got a lot to think about.

This experience has been weird, hard to explain... I almost feel like I've seen my life flash before my eyes in a way.

Superficial shit that seemed so important once, seems less and less significant with every step I take.

CHAPTER SEVENTEEN

Liam

I close the door behind me and lean back against it for a moment, my breathing finally feeling even and relaxed after what seemed like an eternity of arguing and crying – all from Lucia.

It's been hours since Perry left the house, but I know she's still here. She wouldn't let me down by leaving without telling me.

The amount of trust I have in that woman astounds me sometimes.

I've literally handed her my heart, my career, my *everything*. All with a glance.

"Hey stranger, I was starting to think that you'd forgot where your house was."

My eyelids flutter open and just the sight of her, barefoot and relaxed, cements the fact that I did the right thing today.

As hard as it was to sit there and take that abuse from Lucia, and no matter what people might think about it, I did the right thing for *me* – and I think when it comes down to it, that's what April would have wanted. She'd want me to be happy.

"I missed you, freckles."

She smiles sweetly, and I see a look of relief pass over her features. "I missed you too. I was starting to get worried that you'd changed your mind about us."

I hate that she felt like that. I don't want her to doubt my feelings for her for even a fraction of a second.

Lucia might have said some nasty shit to me this afternoon, but there was *nothing* she could have said to make me change my mind about Perry.

Nothing.

Not even losing my job could do that.

"Come here," I say as I close the distance between us.

She sighs a deep breath of relief as she falls against me, our arms entangling around one another.

I breathe her in, right down to my bones. I absorb everything about her, the smell of her skin, the feel of her hair, the way she fits in my arms.

Everything about this woman is perfect in my eyes.

"Was she awful? She seems awful," she asks when I let her go.

I chuckle as I lead her to the couch to sit down.

"Sorry, I know it's horrible to talk about her like that, given what she's been through, but she was so mean to you."

"No need to apologise, she was pretty nasty, there's no real way to sugarcoat it."

I relax into the couch, and Perry snuggles into my side.

She's been watching basketball. That makes me smile. She had no real interest in the sport until I introduced her to it, but now here she is, watching it without me.

"I can't believe she tries to blame you for what happened to April."

Truthfully, I *can* believe it. I had some dark months there myself where I believed the same thing, and for Lucia, it's easier if she has someone to blame – someone to point the finger at.

Her anger is a form of grief, I know that, I do... but it doesn't make it any easier to deal with.

She seems to have forgotten that I'm a victim in this as much as she is.

The only future I'd ever known got wiped out with that accident.

April and I had been talking about settling down in one place, we'd talked about starting a family within the next year. All that was ripped away from me in a matter of minutes.

I realise I've been silent, staring at the screen when she speaks again, her voice soft.

"It wasn't your fault, Liam. Not even a little bit. It's just life. Cruel and unforgiving."

I kiss the top of her head. I know.

"I told them I want a divorce," I blurt out.

"What? *Why*?" She twists around so she can look at me.

"Because I met you," I reply simply.

"Liam," she breathes. "I don't expect you to do that, not because of me."

"I want to do it. I *have* to. I can't live like this anymore, Perry. She doesn't know me, she doesn't want my comfort... It's time to let go. I can't hold on any longer. I've known this had to happen for a few months now, but I never felt ready, not until you."

Her eyes widen and gloss over and her mouth opens, but nothing comes out.

"And then there's also the fact that as long as I'm married to *her*, I can never be married to *you*... I know it's only early days, but I'm pretty confident that's something I'm going to want one day."

"Liam," she whispers, her hand coming up to cover her mouth.

I chuckle nervously. "Sorry, I'm probably coming on a bit strong, but I can't help it with you."

She shakes her head, tears welling in her eyes and lifts her face so she can swipe her lips tenderly against mine.

"You are the most incredible man I've ever met."

"I think your being generous," I murmur as I cup her jaw.

We stare at one another for a long moment, unsaid words passing between us.

"What happens if one day she wakes up and she's April again?" she whispers.

It's a loaded question, and one I've thought about a lot since I met Perry, even though it's an impossible reality.

"She won't."

"But if she did?" she insists.

"Then I'd still be with you. Would it be hard? Yeah, of course it would – but I love you Perry, I'm with *you*."

"Okay," she replies softly as she hears the well-thought-out truth in my voice.

I loved April, I really, truly did, and we were happy together. We would have been happy together for a long time, but I've been forced to move on from that. My feelings have changed. My heart belongs to someone else now.

"Does that make me a terrible person?" I ask her.

She shakes her head. "No, I think it makes you human."

"I promised her until death do us part, in sickness and in health, but I can't do it."

She strokes her hand down my face. "I don't think anyone expects you to stay. She's like a child, Liam. I'm sure she wouldn't want that for you."

I bring her hand up to my mouth and kiss each of her knuckles.

"You were incredible with her."

I'm in total awe of Perry.

I don't know what I did to get so lucky, but the kindness and compassion she showed April today just proves what an unbelievable woman she really is.

"I didn't do anything special."

"You did so much. She talked to you about the stuff she likes. She *liked* you."

"She painted my nails purple and glittery." She giggles and I laugh along with her.

I flip her hand so I can look at the polish adorning each nail.

"Well I like them."

"I kinda do too."

She settles back in against me and her eyes drift back to the TV before returning to me.

"So how did Lucia take the news?"

I blow out a breath and run my hand through my hair. "Not well."

"That doesn't surprise me. And Frank?"

"Got up and shook my hand – told me I was doing the right thing."

She grins. "Maybe we could wait until Lucia was out to visit April again, I actually think I quite like Frank."

I frown at her. "You want to visit again?"

She looks at me as though I've lost my mind. "Of course. I told her I would, and just because she won't be your wife anymore, doesn't mean she's not still your family."

My throat feels thick, and I try to swallow down the lump forming.

Perry notices and her eyes widen. "I mean we'll only go back if you want to, it's not my call, I just thought it would be nice to pop in every once in a while."

"I want to, freckles, I just can't believe you'd be willing to go back there, for me."

She smiles shyly. "Oh c'mon, I'm willing to risk my education for you; visiting your ex-wife is *nothing*." She rolls her eyes, her tone light and teasing.

There's something about her in that moment that makes me lose control, I just have to have her.

I lift her into my lap in a flash, a gasp falling from her lips as she sees the intention in my eyes.

It doesn't take long to see the same hunger reflected back at me.

CHAPTER EIGHTEEN

Perry

"Professor hotty is going to get a total boner when he sees this."

I scowl at her. "Can you *please* refrain from talking about my boyfriend's junk?"

Maddy shakes her head, her eyes trained on the board she's arranging photographs on. "That's a deal I'm just not willing to make."

I huff out a laugh. She's such a pain in the ass.

I still can't quite believe I let her take these shots of me.

I don't know what I was thinking.

Actually, that's a lie. I know *exactly* what I was thinking. I was thinking about Liam seeing them.

I almost feel a little bit guilty for putting temptation right under his nose like that, but I figured it was worth a shot, plus it helped out Maddy – so win, win.

Even if they're incredibly embarrassing.

They're beautiful, tasteful shots, but I'd appreciate them a hell of a lot more if someone else was the main subject.

Maddy will get good marks for her final assessment at least, that much I'm sure of.

These shots were never intended to be graded by anyone other than Liam, but this is her best work, so it made sense for her to explore it further for her end-of-year assessment.

"Damn, P." Trevor whistles low as he strolls into the room and looks over Maddy's shoulder. "That teacher you're banging is a lucky dude."

Maddy thumps him in the shoulder and he grins at her. "What? You did a good job, baby."

"Quit perving on my best friend and don't talk about her boyfriend like that."

That's pretty rich coming from Maddy, who now openly refers to him as 'professor hotty' – even to his face when we're not in class.

"You know you're my number one, Madds." He grins wickedly and nuzzles at her neck.

She loses the frown and smiles along with him.

"P is my number two." He chuckles and darts out of the way as she throws another punch.

"Get out of here you little perve," she grumbles at him as he leaves the room, laughing, not a care in the damn world.

She rolls her eyes, but I see the smile tugging at her lips.

Her and Trevor are so sound, so secure in their relationship and one another, there's no need for jealously or insecurity – it's something I've admired and been envious of for years.

"How's yours going?"

I drop one of her photos and sigh. "It's *so* pretty, I think I might be in love with it, does that make me big-headed?"

"You know, you could hand in a photo of a paper bag and you'd probably still get an 'A', sleeping with the teacher to get good marks is so tasteless of you." She sniggers.

I shove her shoulder. "You're such a bitch." I giggle.

"Seriously though, your work is incredible, if you didn't think so I'd be a little bit concerned about your judgement. You're crazy talented – own that shit."

I am owning that shit.

My final assessment is going to be even better than last year's.

I'm using some of the shots I got with Liam up at Rocky Hill, combined with the shots from all the other locations we've visited.

We're in some of them, but we're totally unrecognisable.

It's like a road trip, my work... it feels like I'm retracing the steps of a journey and I can't help but fall in love with the subject matter all over again every time I look at it.

"Girrrrl, you've got hearts in your eyes."

I shake myself from my trance and grin. "I've turned into one of *those* girls."

"You have, and frankly, it's disgusting." She smirks as she starts tossing her stuff into a box. "We better get going, P, not all of us have girlfriend-teacher privileges, and I can't afford to be late again."

I snort a laugh at her and point to the at least half a dozen other things she's forgotten that she'll need.

She groans and tosses them in the box too before shrugging on her coat.

I grab my bag off the couch and sling it over my shoulder.

"You still haven't told me how it went with the wife," she reminds me as we head out the door. "Later, babe!" she hollers out to Trevor.

I pull the door closed behind us and wrap my coat a little tighter around my body.

I can't say I'll miss the walk to campus every day once we graduate. There's only a few weeks left until the end of the semester, then another month until graduation and then everything will change.

I don't know where I'll be living or working, but I do know one thing, I'll be doing it with Liam in my life – and not just behind closed doors.

"So spill," Maddy encourages as we fall into step. "Was it weird meeting his old wife and her family?"

"It was something alright," I mutter.

"What's Liam like with her?"

I mull it over in my head for a bit, trying to think of the right word. "Hesitant," I finally say. "Kinda how you might be with a child who doesn't know you."

As awful as it sounds – that's exactly how it is.

"That really sucks," she says, "I mean it's obviously not a bad thing for you, because now you get him –"

"Maddy!"

"Oh *whatever*, you know what I mean." She rolls her eyes. "If he was still happily married, then you never would have got together."

It's a strange concept – to think that I would have felt this attraction but not have been able to do anything about it.

I might be willing to break the rules as far as a student-teacher relationship goes, but I'm no home wrecker, and Liam isn't a cheat.

This is hands down the most complex relationship I've ever found myself in.

"Her mum was a complete bitch to Liam."

I probably shouldn't be talking about it, but I feel the urge to be a girl my age for five minutes and have a good old-fashioned vent session to my best friend.

"Yeah?" she asks in surprise.

I nod. "She blames him for the whole accident. She had a few digs about him moving on with me –"

"Oh, what does she expect? Him to just live alone with his blue balls forever?" she interrupts me.

I can't help but laugh at that. You can always rely on Maddy to say something inappropriate.

"He told them he wants a divorce."

She grabs my arm and forces us to stop. "I'm sorry, what now?"

I can't help the smile spreading across my face as I nod. "I know."

"Oh my god, P, this guy is really serious about you."

I nod again. I feel like jumping up and down with excitement. "I asked him why, and he said it was time, and that if he was married to her, he could never be married to me."

Her eyes widen and a shriek leaves her mouth.

"Oh my god, shhhh," I hiss at her, "you're making a scene."

"And you're going to marry professor hotty."

I tug her so she'll start walking again; the last thing we need is to be late on top of her being so animated.

"Calm down, it's not like he proposed, but oh my god, my heart literally stopped beating when he said that."

"You two are end game. I'm calling it right now." She grins at me. "I'm going to be your maid of honour one day and I'm going to babysit your kids. This is going to be so fun. Imagine how pretty your babies will be."

"You need to calm down."

"You need to start looking at engagement rings." She points her finger at me.

I shake my head in amusement. "Seriously, *stop*. I think we should worry about making our relationship public before we even go anywhere near getting engaged."

We approach the building our photography studio is in, and I tug open the door.

The warm air engulfs us, and I cast a warning glance at Maddy.

Anyone could hear us now, and I need her to remember that.

She makes a zipping action over her lips, and I shake my head at her antics.

We walk side by side to our class, and when I open the door and my gaze lands on Liam, my heart skips a beat.

CHAPTER NINETEEN

Liam

The door shuts and I have her pressed up against it before she can even speak.

"It's getting harder and harder to keep my hands off you in class," I growl against her throat before nipping at the soft skin there.

She moans and drops her bag to the floor, her head falling back in pleasure.

I run my hands up her front and slide her coat off her shoulders.

Her hands find my shirt and tug it from my jeans, her fingers making quick work of the buttons.

"I know the feeling," she murmurs as I trail kisses up her neck to her ear.

I reach for the hem of her jersey and tug it over her head, my lips finding hers in a frenzy.

My shirt is hanging open in the front and the feel of her skin on mine only spurs me into action further.

I hoist her up by her ass and her back hits the door again with a soft thud, her legs coming around my waist.

"All day I've fantasised about this body."

"So you just want me for my body?" she says, a cheeky grin on her face.

"I was attracted to your beauty first, I won't lie, but you know what really sucked me in?"

"What?" she whispers.

"The way that you look at a photograph, the way you see the world through a lens. Your beauty pulled me in, but your talent, Perry, that's what's held me."

She nibbles on her lip, and it takes every ounce of my control not to suck that lip into my mouth. Her hands roam over my abdomen and she sighs heavily. "I need you, click."

She looks so fucking perfect in her white lace bra, her dark wavy hair falling to her shoulders.

I grind myself against her, and she moans a sexy, breathy moan.

I feel her tugging on my belt buckle between us, and I spin her around so I can sit her on the hall table.

I've just about got my belt off when there's a sharp knock at the door.

"Shit," I mutter.

I didn't buzz anyone up, so if they've made it this far, it means it's likely to be someone I know.

Someone that *shouldn't* know about me and Perry.

Perry's eyes widen and she scrambles down from the table.

I hold up my finger to my lips in a gesture telling her to be quiet.

She scampers around grabbing her clothes from the floor as I do up the buttons on my shirt and will my hard-on to go down.

Whoever's at the door knocks again.

I point to the bedroom and she runs down the hallway.

I can't help but grin, sneaking around is exciting sometimes.

"I'm coming!" I yell out as I do up the final button and tuck my shirt back into my jeans.

I've got no idea if I look presentable or not, but I'm out of time.

I unlock the door and swing it open.

"Oh hey," I say when I see Linc standing on the other side of the door.

This could be awkward if he's come over to watch a game or something; I can't just leave Perry locked in the bedroom until he leaves.

I glance at his hands, but they're missing the usual box of beers he'd be carrying if that was the case.

"Hey," he replies tightly.

That's when I really look at him.

Something's wrong.

This isn't a social visit. Not even close.

My stomach drops.

I can only think of *one* thing that would make him look at me with the disappointment he is now.

"Are you alright?" I ask cautiously.

He gives me a pained look. "Why don't *you* tell *me*?"

I chuckle nervously. "What do you mean?"

He sighs. "Save it, Liam, I've just got off the phone with Lucia."

Fuck.

"Linc..."

"Imagine my surprise when she told me that you're divorcing April, because you've got a new girlfriend."

"I can explain –"

"But that surprise was *nothing* on learning that your new woman's name was Perry." He carries on, ignoring my protests.

My head falls forward in defeat.

Shit. He knows everything.

I should have known Lucia would talk.

"Did you tell her that Perry was a student?" I ask.

"Jesus, it's *true*?" he demands.

I nod. "Did you tell her?" I repeat my question. I need to know if he's given Lucia the information she could use to really hurt us.

"I was too in shock to tell her anything." He groans. "I didn't want to believe it, I thought Lucia was being crazy again, but fuck, Liam, what the hell are you thinking?"

I step aside and gesture for him to come inside so we can discuss this in private. The last thing I need is the whole floor hearing our argument.

He storms inside, paces into the living room then comes charging back out. "I can't believe you'd be this stupid. She's your student, you *do* understand that, right?"

"I know."

"And yet you did it anyway. Jesus Christ, tell me you haven't slept with her?" He rubs his temples in frustration.

I blow out a deep breath but before I can answer he groans again.

Obviously my face is telling the story without words.

"This is worse than I thought, and trust me, what I thought was pretty fucking bad."

"I didn't plan for this to happen, it just did."

"Oh it *just did*? Well that makes it so much fucking better," he replies sarcastically.

He's pacing the room back and forth, and I can't think of what to say to make this better.

"You have to end it. *Right now*. Classes will be over in a few weeks and she'll move on and you'll never have to see her again."

"Linc –"

"Just ditch her and forget she ever existed," he carries on, muttering away to himself like he's formulating some kind of plan in his head.

"That's *not* going to fucking happen." My tone is gruff, yet eerily firm.

The words are out of my mouth before I've even had the chance to think them through, but I don't regret them.

What he's saying is *wrong*. Far more wrong than two consenting adults being together, no matter what anyone else might say.

"*What*?" he demands.

"I'm not going to discard her like a toy I've used and got bored of. She's better than that and so am I."

"She's just a piece of ass, bro, a hot one – I'll give you that, but you can't risk your career, your *reputation* for some chick."

I've got him by the scruff of the neck, his back pressed against the wall before he even finishes his sentence.

"Don't *ever* fucking talk about her like that again," I growl.

His eyes widen in surprise. "Are you serious right now? You're going at me? *Me*? Your best mate... after everything we've been through, you're going to threaten me over some chick you're banging?"

I force him against the wall even harder.

"She's not *some chick*." I sneer the words at him. "Her name is Perry, and I'm not just 'fucking' her, I'm in love with her."

He sucks in a breath and it hits me then, exactly what I'm doing.

I'm about thirty seconds away from getting into a punch-up with my closest friend.

My fist slowly unclenches, and I step back, staring at my own hand like it doesn't belong to me.

"You *love* her?"

I stare at him as though he's not even speaking English anymore.

"Do. You. Love. Her?" he demands, talking to me like I'm stupid.

I nod slowly, the reality of my life sinking in.

He *knows*.

I'm with Perry and he knows about it.

He could destroy me with this knowledge – more importantly, he could destroy *her*, and after the way I just treated him, I wouldn't even blame him for doing exactly that.

"I'm sorry."

"For what? For hooking up with a student or for roughing me up like some kind of street kid?"

I meet his eyes.

"I'm sorry that I've put you in this position, I'm sorry that I put my hands on you... but I'm not sorry for her, not even a little bit."

"You're really willing to lose your job for her?" he asks, his expression one of disbelief.

"If that's what has to happen, then yeah, I am."

He huffs out a breath. "I don't know what the fuck has gotten into you, man."

I shrug my shoulders. I'm not sure I do either.

"The Liam I knew would never have crossed the line like this."

"Well maybe I'm not the Liam you knew anymore. I changed after that crash, not the way April did, but I'm not the same anymore either. How could I be?"

He looks at me with a pained expression, and it's obvious how much he really does care about me – I know he has my best interests at heart, but I'm not going to stand back and let him disrespect the woman I've fallen in love with.

"Can't you just be happy for us?"

He holds my gaze for a beat before blowing out a breath and dropping his eyes to the floor. "If it weren't a student, I'd be over the moon for you, you know that. But this... I don't support this. I can't."

"She's not going to be my student for much longer, it's like you said, classes will be over in a few weeks and then we'll be free to do whatever we want."

"Was that your plan then? Wait until the year was over and then pretend you'd just got together? Lie to me forever?"

"I wanted to tell you, but I was worried you'd fucking react exactly like you are right now."

"How am I supposed to react?" he demands, his voice rising.

I shake my head and huff out a breath. "I don't know, man, I really don't fucking know, but I didn't want to put you in this position, that's why I didn't tell you – not because I didn't want you to know."

He paces the room again, this time stopping in front of the door.

"What are you going to do now?" I ask carefully, my voice measured.

He shakes his head, his back to me. "I don't know."

I nod, my heart thumping against my rib cage. "Fair enough."

"Just so you know, I'm glad you're going ahead with a divorce, I know you loved her, but it's time."

"It is," I agree.

"But you've screwed me over here, Liam. I'm stuck between a rock and a hard place. This isn't just your career, it's mine too."

"You do what you have to do, I understand," I tell him calmly.

He nods once, opens the door, and then he's gone.

"Fuck!" I roar. I swipe the stack of books from the benchtop and they go flying to the floor.

Everything is all fucked up, and I don't know what the hell I'm meant to do now.

I rake my hands over my face in frustration.

Perry would have heard every word of that, and she's probably ready to run a mile the first chance she gets.

I can't lose her.

Not now.

Not over this.

I take a deep breath.

This happening has made a few things clear to me. I know what I want, without *any* doubt.

Now I just need to know if she feels the same way.

CHAPTER TWENTY

Perry

He comes into the bedroom quietly, his expression broken, and I'm not surprised after what just went down out there.

I feel *so* guilty for my part in all of this.

This isn't how Linc should have found out about us and our relationship.

Liam should have been able to tell him in his own time, on his own terms.

I hate Lucia from taking that from him, but I hate *myself* more for letting this happen to him.

This is my fault. I'm the reason he could lose his job *and* his best friend. Being with me has messed everything up for him.

I wouldn't blame him for walking away from me after that, it would hurt like hell, but I'd understand. He probably thinks I'm the worst decision he's ever made.

I swipe the tear rolling down my cheek as our eyes meet.

He pauses in the doorway and the look he gives me melts my heart and scares off my insecurities in nothing more than a fraction of a second.

I can still see the love in his eyes. It's shining as bright as the sun. He still loves me, despite everything.

Relief floods my body.

He still loves me.

I rush forward and wrap my arms around his middle. "Liam, I'm so, so sorry."

He clears his throat but doesn't speak, he just holds me, and I hold him back just as tight. I think he's feeling as emotional about this as I am.

In this moment it feels like all we have is one another, even though I know that's not true, the way he's clinging to me like a lifeline makes me feel otherwise.

He strokes my hair, my waist, his hands exploring everything from my ass to the top of my head.

When he does speak, he says the last thing I could ever have imagined would come out of his mouth after what just went down.

"Move in with me after graduation."

"*What*?" I whisper in shock.

He holds me at arm's length and stares right into my eyes. "I want you to move in with me."

"But... but, *why*? After what just happened... I thought... I didn't know... What if you lose your job because of me?"

He chuckles at my rambling. "Breathe, freckles."

"But what about Lincoln?"

"What about him?" he asks as though the answer doesn't really matter. But I know better – I know he'll be crushed if he doesn't find a way to make things right with Lincoln.

"He's your best friend, and he was really, really angry. He might tell the university, and then what will you have?"

He's quiet for a few beats as the reality of our situation settles in.

"I hope I'll still have you?" he asks, his voice cracking with emotion.

He thinks I'm going to run.

"*Liam*," I breathe. "*Of course* you have me." I tug him into my arms. "I'm yours, I'm here. I'm not going anywhere."

"Then the rest doesn't matter," he replies, voice muffled against my shoulder. "It'll all work itself out... or it won't. I can live with it either way, but I don't want to live without you, Perry."

I press my lips against his stubbly jaw.

"You really want me to live with you?"

He nods, his expression tender. "Unless you've got somewhere else you'd rather be?"

I think about that for a second. I want to be wherever he is. I know that for certain. I might not be sure of anything else in regard to my future, but I know whatever it is, he'll be in it.

"I can't think of a single place."

His hand runs down the side of my face, and I find myself biting my lip to stop myself going all breathy and needy.

I can't believe this is happening.

I can't believe this sexy, sweet man is mine.

I can't believe he loves me the way I love him.

I can't believe he sees a future for us the same way I do.

"Did you hear those fucking awful things he said about you out there?"

I nod. I heard it all, but I'm not mad, I couldn't possibly be when I know he was just trying to look out for Liam.

"He didn't mean that shit, it wasn't personal, I need you to know that – that was about me, not about you."

"I know. But honestly, I don't care if it was personal. Sure, I want your friends to like me, I *do*, but the only person whose validation I need about our relationship, is yours, click."

"I'm glad to hear that," he whispers.

His mouth is so close to mine, I can feel his breath fanning across my face.

"Now, where were we before he interrupted?"

"I think you were just about to do some laundry?" I tease.

"You're right. I need those clothes you're wearing, mine too – we better take them all off."

I giggle as he grabs the waistband of my jeans and tugs me against him, his hardness obvious.

"Can't go and get behind on laundry now, can we?"

"No, we *can't*," I murmur as he crushes his mouth to mine so we can pick up right where we left off.

***

I slip out of his room, grinning to myself. It'll be *our* room in only a few more weeks.

I still can't quite believe it.

Maddy is going to shit the bed when I tell her about it.

I can already hear her squeals ringing in my ears.

I grab an apple from the fruit bowl before I leave the apartment. I have to shoot home, get changed and get to the uni before classes start.

I know I told Liam that I didn't need validation from Lincoln, and I'm still not sure that I do, but I know that I lay awake last night for hours, listening to Liam's peaceful breathing in and out, and decided that I couldn't do nothing.

As awkward and inappropriate as it might be, I need to talk to Lincoln. I need him to know what this relationship means to Liam – what it means to *me*.

It could blow up in my face and send him running straight to the dean, but at least I'll know I tried.

I don't think I could live with myself if Liam got fired and I didn't do anything.

I know there's a chance I could get kicked out of my course for this and not be able to graduate, but I'm trying not to think too much about that.

Last year, if someone had told me that I'd risk my future for a guy, I would have laughed in their face, but now, although I still have a passion for photography and a burning desire to explore it as a career, I also have Liam. And I undoubtably know which one takes priority.

I climb into my car, start the engine and crank the heater onto high as I pull out and drive the short distance back to my flat.

When I walk in, surprisingly, I can hear Maddy already out of bed.

I can also smell pancakes, so I guess that's how Trevor lured her out – he's a smart man that one.

"Morning!" I call out as I hang my coat up.

"Check you, girl, rolling in wearing yesterday's clothes," Maddy teases as I stroll into the kitchen and sit down at the bench next to her.

"Guilty as charged."

"Did you get caught up in the throes of passion and then fall asleep from all the sex?"

I burst into laughter. "Um, yeah something like that. It was kind of a start, stop then start again kind of thing... then it was late and I couldn't be bothered coming home."

"Don't tell me he had to stop to pop a pill." Trevor chuckles. "I knew he was older, but damn."

I frown at him in confusion and he gestures with a bent, limp-looking finger in front of his crotch.

"Oh, for the love of god, Trevor, no! I'll have you know there are no problems in that area."

Maddy giggles. "Good to know."

Trevor offers me a pancake, and I nod eagerly.

"Mr. Radcliff turned up at Liam's... you remember him from first year?"

She nods.

"He and Liam are good friends, and he found out about us."

"Oh shit." She winces.

"Mmm hmm." I nod. "It wasn't pretty."

"Fuck, so what happens now?"

I shrug. "I'm going to go and talk to him this morning."

"Ummmm." She grimaces. "I might not have any experience with secret relationships, but that seems like an awfully bad idea."

"Probably," I agree before stuffing some of the pancake in my mouth.

"But you're going to do it anyway, aren't you?"

I nod. "Sure am."

"Wear something sexy, so at least you'll look good when it all turns to shit," she offers helpfully.

"That's a good idea, I'll be sure to do that," I reply with a roll of my eyes.

I get to my feet. I still need to shower, get changed and get to campus.

"Oh, Trev," I pause in the doorway, "I was wondering how you'd feel about having her to yourself in the not-too-distant future?" I tip my head in Maddy's direction.

Trevor chuckles. "I've done an alright job of keeping her alive so far, so sure, why not?"

"Good, because when I move in with Liam after graduation, she's going to be *all* yours."

"Whaaaaaat?" Maddy shrieks.

I giggle all the way to my room with her hot on my heels *demanding* the gossip.

CHAPTER TWENTY-ONE

Liam

I grin to myself as I read her note again.

I've gone to class... I didn't want to wake you, you were snoring, and as obnoxious as it was, I can't wait to hear it every night.
I love you,
P x

I stretch my arms above my head and yawn loudly, I haven't slept that well in a while, so as much as it sucks I didn't get to see her face and kiss her lips before she took off, I'm glad she left me to sleep. I needed it.

As messed up as it is, having Linc know my secret is a weight off my shoulders. I didn't realise how much tension I was holding from keeping this from him.

I have no idea what he's going to do with the information he's got, but I won't judge him regardless. He's got a wife and family at home, and he's right, I *have* put his career in jeopardy. He got me the job, so his reputation is on the line like mine is.

I just hope we can still be mates when this has blown over.

We've been through a lot, and I would hate to lose him from my life.

Him and Nicky have been so good to me.

I glance at the time on the clock, I've only got one class today, and it's not for a couple of hours, so the morning is all mine.

I sit up on the side of the bed and grin again as the note drifts to the ground.

There's just something about that woman.

I get to my feet, in all my naked glory, and head for the shower.

I've decided that apartment living isn't so bad after all, you can walk around nude and there's no nosey neighbour peering into your window.

I need to talk to Perry about whether she wants to stay here or not next year. I know I just dropped the 'move in' bomb on her last night, but the more I've been thinking about it, the more I think we should get out there and live.

This cosy apartment will always be here for us when we come back.

I turn the shower on and step under the steady, steaming hot stream.

There are so many beautiful things in the world that neither of us have ever seen, and I want to be there to watch her see them all. I want to watch her raise her camera and see the evidence of the world through her eyes.

I reach for the soap and my memory flicks back to the way Perry looked in this very shower last night, the water washing over her hair and trailing down her body, over her hard nipples and all the way down those long, sexy legs.

I can picture her sprawled out beneath me, her legs wide, her finger beckoning me to come closer.

Fuck, I can still remember the way she tastes.

I groan, my head falling forward as I remember the noises she made as I slipped inside her and took her to the point of pleasure she was so desperately seeking.

Fuck.

I'm hard as a rock just thinking about it.

I take myself in my hand and stroke gently, once, twice, and then again, faster and faster until I'm crying out in ecstasy.

"Jesus Christ, Perry," I groan.

That woman has the ability to do wicked things to me, even when she's not around.

I let the water beat down on me, washing away any evidence of arousal until my stomach is rumbling.

***

I rub my hair dry with a fresh, white towel, another slung low around my hips as I stroll out into the kitchen in search of food.

My cell rings shrill and loud from where I've left it on the hall table, and I jog over to get it.

I'm expecting Perry, so when I see Nicky's name on the screen, my throat feels thick all of a sudden.

I don't know what my best mate's wife is calling for, but it's not likely to be anything good.

Nicky is as much of a friend to me as Linc is – we've known each other a long time now, we go way back, and we've all supported each other through a lot.

I know it wasn't easy for Nicky to watch what happened to April any more than it was for me.

"Hey, Nic," I answer.

"Hey, Liam, how are you doing?"

I blow out a breath and pad back towards the kitchen. Food might have to wait, but coffee doesn't.

"Do you want the honest answer or the generic one?"

She huffs out a laugh. "From you? The honest one. Always."

"I've been better."

I tuck the phone against my ear with my shoulder as I fill the coffee machine and hit the start button.

"Linc told me everything."

I sigh. I knew he would, but I'm not sure I'm ready for another 'what were you thinking' lecture just yet.

"Look, Nicky, you know I love you, and I'm sure you're disappointed in me and all, but is it really so bad? She's nearly twenty-one, it's not like I've groomed some seventeen-year-old student and forced her into my bed, I mean *shit*... we're both adults, and yeah, the circumstances are less than ideal, but that will all change soon and then we'll just be two people in love."

She's quiet for a minute.

"I just wanted to hear it for myself," she finally says.

I rub at my brow. "Hear what?"

"Hear you say that you're in love with her... I just want you to be happy, Liam, after everything you've been through, I think you deserve that much. Do I wish you'd waited until you were in the clear? Yeah, of course I do, but it's too late now for should have, and if this woman is what you want, then I'll support you, no matter what."

My heart swells with her words. "I wish your husband felt the same way," I grumble, even though I have no right.

"Give him time," she soothes.

Linc has always been the hot head in their relationship. He's always gone in, all guns blazing, where Nicky is calmer and more rational. She thinks things through before she reacts.

"I don't think time is going to help on this one, Nic. I crossed the line."

I can hear her pacing the room. "I'm not going to lie to you, he tossed and turned all night."

I feel bad for that, I really do. It hits me like a blow to the chest. Here I am, sleeping like a baby with Perry curled up against me, and Linc is suffering away.

I haven't been a very good friend.

"Give him a day or two to process, and then try and talk to him. It'll be good to clear the air, regardless of what he decides to do."

"I won't blame him, you know that, right? If he has to tell the university, then that's okay with me. I made my choice when I chose her, and now he has to make his."

"I know you won't," she replies softly, and I can hear the smile in her tone. "You might have made a questionable decision, but you're a good mate, Liam – and everything you've done has been for love, that much has never changed about you and you should be proud. I know April would be."

I feel all choked up all of a sudden. "Thanks, Nic." I clear my throat. "I better get going, but thanks for calling, it means a lot to me.

"It was nothing," she replies, "And once all this dust settles, I'd really like to meet her, okay? She must be quite the woman."

"She certainly is."

CHAPTER TWENTY-TWO

Perry

I raise my hand to knock on the door of the graphics design suite but hesitate.

Maybe Maddy was right after all and this was a really, *really* bad idea.

Mr. Radcliff is on the other side of this door, and if his mood is anything like it was at Liam's last night, then it's bound to be an unpleasant visit.

That thought takes me back to Liam and the hurt look in his eyes after he argued with his best mate, and I know I'm doing the right thing by trying to clear the air.

Linc might have said some cutting things about me last night, but he doesn't know me. Not at all, but that's going to change if we're both going to be in Liam's life – so now is as good of a time as any to get started building a bridge between us.

I rap my knuckles against the wooden door.

"Come in," his deep voice calls back to me.

I push open the door, take a deep breath, and step inside.

He turns away from the computer and does a double take when he sees me standing in his classroom.

"Perry, right? I'm not sure you should be here."

"Please, Mr. Radcliff –"

"Call me Linc," he interrupts me and runs his hand through his hair in obvious frustration. "For the love of god, you're sleeping with my best mate, I think we're past the formalities."

"Linc, then," I reply softly as I take a few slow steps into the room. "I just wanted to talk to you about Liam."

"You can stop right there because I bet I can already guess what you're going to say."

I shrug at him. Maybe he can, maybe he can't, but I'm damn well going to say it anyway.

"I'm not here to try and talk you in or out of anything, we know what we're doing is against the rules, and if you need to report us to keep your conscience clear, then so be it."

His brow furrows as he listens to me speak. He looks surprised... confused. He obviously thought I was here to beg for his silence.

"Neither of us are going to judge you for it, and honestly, I'm sorry we ever put you in this position. It wasn't fair of either of us."

He nods once in silent appreciation. He doesn't say anything, so I take that as my cue to carry on.

"I just wanted you to know that no matter what, even if he gets fired and I can't graduate, I'm still not giving him up. This isn't some fling or stupid crush. I *love* Liam, I love him even more since I found out about the state of his life. So I just thought you should know that I'll be there by his side no matter what, and no matter who tries to tell us this is wrong – because honestly, when I'm with him, it's the most right thing in my life."

I don't even know if he knows he's doing it, but he's nodding slowly, over and over.

"That was some speech," he finally says.

I shrug. "I guess I better get to class, I just figured that I heard what you had to say, so you should have to hear what I have to say too."

I turn to leave but he calls out to me.

"What do you mean, you heard what I had to say?"

"I was at Liam's last night. I heard the two of you arguing."

"*Shit*." His eyes drop to the floor. "Look, I said some things last night... some things I'm not proud of. Some things my wife threatened to slap me for actually."

That gets a small smile out of me.

He glances back up at me. "I'm sorry I talked about you like you were just some chick he'd taken to bed and should throw away like last night's leftovers."

He's genuinely apologetic, I can see that. And I'm glad – I really want to get along with Linc – I know how important he is to Liam.

"It's okay. You kinda had the whole thing sprung on you, you weren't to know it was anything more than that."

I take another few steps towards the door before he stops me again. "He really loves you, you know? I can see it in his eyes. I haven't seen him look like that in a long time, and even though I don't approve of what you both are involved in, I'm glad he's found something real with you."

He really is a good man.

"Thank you, *really*... that means a lot, especially given the complicated situation."

"And for what it's worth, I hope you two can make it work because seeing him happy again is all I've ever wanted."

"You're a good friend."

"Am I though?" he questions me. "Even though I'm considering dobbing him in?"

I shrug. "Even then. I meant what I said, Linc, no one will judge you – we put you in this position and we understand that you'll do what you think is right. Just don't push him away as a friend. I know he loves you, and he needs you in his life."

I get out the door this time, he doesn't speak again, but I feel his eyes on my back the entire way.

CHAPTER TWENTY-THREE

Liam

I watch as the last student files out of my year two photography class and pulls the door almost shut behind him.

That class felt like it took *forever*. It was lucky I only had the one today, I'm not sure my brain could have coped with anything more, even after a full night's sleep.

I've only got one thing I can focus on with any sort of enthusiasm right now, and that's getting packed up and getting over to Perry's place so I can wrap her in my arms.

She's the best medicine for me, the only thing that can truly soothe my soul.

Lucia has called me twice today, but I've let them both go to voicemail. I'm not sure I can be trusted to speak to her with any type of respect right now, and I don't want to stoop to that level. April might not be the woman I married anymore, but I want to honour her by treating her mother the way I always did when we were together.

I shut down my laptop and disconnect the cables running to the big screen I had a slideshow playing on during class.

Someone clearing their throat behind me startles me, and I spin around to see who's there.

"Hey," he says.

"Hey," I repeat back awkwardly.

Lincoln is the last person I expected to show up in my classroom at the end of the day.

We stand there in silence, both looking at one another and contemplating what to say next.

For all I know, he's here to tell me that I've lost my job, and that Perry isn't going to get to graduate. Given that it's him here and not my superiors, I'm fairly certain he hasn't said a word yet, but the idea of her not getting to wear that gown and cap causes my stomach to sink.

He opens his mouth to speak, but I get in first.

"Can I just ask you for one favour? Even though you don't owe it to me?"

He nods, indicating for me to continue.

"If you haven't already, when you go to the dean, can you leave Perry's name out of it? I don't care what happens to me, but if she loses the chance to graduate, I won't be able to live with myself."

He's watching me curiously, but he doesn't say a word.

"Linc, c'mon, man, just tell them you saw me with a student, but you don't know who it was. I've never asked you to lie for me before – well not since that time in first year where I got too drunk and didn't turn up to class – but I need you to lie for me now. To protect her. That's all I care about," I beg.

"She's the real deal, huh?"

I frown at him. I don't know what he's getting at, and he still hasn't answered my question. "What are you talking about?"

"She came to see me," he explains.

"She *what*?" I balk.

This could have gone one of two ways – Linc is notorious for getting his back up, and if Perry gave him an earful, I doubt he would have taken it well.

He nods. "First thing this morning..."

I wait with bated breath to see what he's going to say next.

"I can see why you like her so much; she's seems pretty fucking cool." The corners of his mouth turn up into a small smile.

I huff out a laugh. "She charmed you?"

He shrugs. "She just gave it to me straight. She's really into you, Liam – that girl has got it bad for you."

"The feeling is completely mutual," I reply honestly. There's no point in lying about how deep I'm in anymore.

"So you're really serious about this then?" he questions.

I nod. "After what happened to April, I never thought I'd see a future in anything again, not a real one anyway, but when I look at Perry, I don't just see a future, I see my whole life right there in front of me."

He chuckles and dips his head. "What the fuck is happening to us? Talking about feelings and shit? I don't even know us anymore."

It's clear he's feeling as emotional about all of this as I am.

I laugh along with him, shaking my head to try and snap out of this deep and meaningful funk. "Tell me about it."

"You finished for the day?"

I nod. "Yeah, I was just going to head over to Perry's, but if you want to grab a beer or something, I can flick her a text?"

He looks at me with his brow furrowed. "You're not even going to ask me if I snitched on you or not?"

I shake my head. "I've told you, man, it's not going to change things between us, it's none of my business..."

"I haven't, not yet anyway."

I nod. "You think you could keep her name out of it when you do?"

I can see he's thinking about it, and I don't miss the small nod he gives me.

"Thanks," I reply gratefully. It's a huge weight off my shoulders. "So how about that beer?"

***

I swing open the door and grin at the two people on the other side.

"Lee-Lee!" Nicky cries, throwing herself into my arms.

"You make me sound like an eight-year-old girl with pigtails when you call me that." I chuckle.

She releases me with a grin. "And that's precisely why I do it."

I hold my hand out to Linc and he shakes it firmly. "Thanks for coming, man, we really appreciate it."

"No sweat," he replies, his grin relaxed and easy as he brushes past me to come inside the apartment.

I'm beyond glad that we seemed to have moved past the awkwardness those couple of days brought.

I hear Perry laugh loudly from the living room, and I can't help the smile that spreads across my face.

Maddy and Trevor are already here, all of us together to celebrate Perry's birthday.

She bursts into the kitchen, laughter still falling from her lips, the locket I gave her fastened around her neck. Just the sight of her makes me fall a little bit deeper in love.

Her eyes dart around from me, to Linc to Nicky.

"Oh hey, you're here," she says, her cheeks pinking.

She sidles up to me and I wrap my arm around her waist.

I know she's nervous about meeting Nicky and hanging out with Linc in a more personal setting.

It's been a trying few days, so I don't blame her for feeling apprehensive.

"Perry, this is Nicky, Nicky, this is my Perry."

Perry giggles.

"I meant my girlfriend, Perry." I chuckle.

"I'm happy to be your Perry." She beams up at me.

Nicky rushes forward and pulls Perry in for a hug. "It's so good to meet you," she says.

Perry giggles. "You too."

"Seeing him so happy... I just can't thank you enough." I hear Nicky's hushed words, but I pretend I don't as I untangle my arm from their embrace and head towards the fridge.

"Beer?" I offer Linc.

He nods as he watches the girls who now seem to be talking about the dress Perry is wearing.

"So, twenty-one, huh?" Linc says as he uncaps the bottle I've handed him.

I chuckle. "I think twenty-one might have been a good year for us."

"Margaritas on the beach for two weeks straight, if I remember right?"

"Don't ask me, I don't remember anything from those two weeks."

"On account of all the margaritas," Nicky cuts in.

Perry giggles. "Someone better get me another drink then; it sounds like I have some making up to do."

Nicky erupts into laughter. "Oh my god, remember that night that April had way too many and –" she stops speaking abruptly as she realises what she's just said, her face falling instantly. "I'm so sorry, I didn't mean to bring her up."

I watch Perry with interest to see how she responds.

Her smile doesn't even falter. She waves off Nicky's horrified expression. "Oh c'mon, I'm *dying* to know what she did."

I take her hand in mine and squeeze it gently. She really is an amazing woman.

Linc and Nicky exchange a glance that doesn't go unnoticed by me, then Nicky finishes her story about April ditching her bikini top and climbing to the top of a coconut tree, until we're all cracking up.

"Come into the living room and meet Maddy and Trevor," Perry tells Linc and Nicky.

"In a sec." Linc reaches out and lightly grips Perry's wrist as she goes to pass him. "I wanted to give you your birthday present first."

Perry eyes him curiously. "Alright..."

He glances from Perry, to me, to Nicky and back to Perry. "I'm not going to tell anyone about the two of you."

My heart pounds against my chest rapidly. I know I would have given it all up for her, but if he's being honest right now, then I won't have to.

"Seriously?" Perry questions.

He half-shrugs, half-nods. "Seriously."

"Thank you!" she shrieks as she throws her arms around his neck and hugs him.

"Woah, woah, woah." He chuckles as he stands there awkwardly half hugging her back.

"Thank you so much." She grins at Linc before looking at me with her eyes shining bright. "I have to go tell Maddy," she cries and runs off to the living room.

Nicky follows after her and leaves the two of us alone.

"You're sure?" I question warily.

I'd never ask this of him, he knows that.

He nods. "I decided I could live with one little break of the rules, but if something happened to you and Perry or to me and you, then I'm not sure I could live with that."

"Thank you," I say, my voice thick.

"No problem." He nods as the girls all start high-pitch giggling and shrieking from the living room about how pretty and shiny something is. I'm guessing Perry just showed them the locket.

We wince at the same time.

"But, Liam?" he says as I head for the noise.

I look back at him over my shoulder.

"You owe me." He smirks.

EPILOGUE

Liam

She crosses the stage, her graduation cap and gown adorning the beautiful body that I'm lucky enough to get to worship every night.

I clap loudly when they hand her the graduation certificate but resist the urge to get to my feet and cheer like the proud-as-fuck boyfriend I am.

We've kept this thing under wraps this long, I don't want to go and blow it now.

I'll give her a private celebration later. Much, much, later.

I'm so glad this day is finally here.

Not only am I not her teacher anymore, but I'm not a teacher at all.

This was only ever a short-term fill-in role, but when they offered me a position for next year, the answer couldn't have been more obvious to me.

I've loved this semester, and I think that teaching is something I want to come back to one day in the future, but for right now, I want to go back to travelling the world and seeing things other people can only dream of – the woman I love at my side.

There's so much more I want to see and experience.

Now that I'm in this place in my life, I can look back fondly at the time April and I spent travelling together, instead of thinking about it with pain-tinted glasses.

We grew so much as individuals *and* as a couple, and I want Perry to experience that too.

She deserves it. We both do.

A big part of me still wants to settle down and start a family, but there's plenty of time for that – it's one of the perks of being with a younger woman – we've got all the time in the world.

"Are you tearing up?" Linc nudges my leg, his grin wide and infectious as Perry disappears from the stage.

"You wish." I chuckle, my tone hushed.

We're both seated on the stage with the rest of the faculty.

"You must be proud though," he says, more genuinely this time.

"You've got no idea." I blow out a breath. "I'm also really fucking relieved, man, I'm not going to lie. This day has been a long time coming."

"For you and me both." He chuckles. "I suck with secrets."

"Well for what it's worth, I appreciate it. We both do."

He clears his throat as a woman in the row in front of us turns around to glare at us for talking.

I grin at Linc. Some things never change. We used to get in trouble for the same shit when we were students.

Linc holds his hands up in apology.

I glance around and find Perry now seated in the front row, her certificate clasped in her hands and her eyes focused solely on me.

I don't think I'll ever get sick of seeing that look in her eyes.

"I love you," I mouth to her.

She smiles shyly and blushes before going back to watching the other students getting their certificates.

Linc leans in closer. "So while we're talking about me keeping your secrets, you remember how I said you owed me?"

I groan and nod. "It's ringing a bell."

"Good, because I'm cashing in my favour," he drawls.

"What do you want?"

"So, you know how we went to school with that total ass-kiss of a dude who's wound up shooting photos for those 'sexy' calendars?"

I narrow my eyes. "I'm familiar, yes."

"Well he contacted me the other day and asked me to be part of next year's."

A loud laugh slips out and the woman turns and scowls at us again.

"Sorry," I whisper.

She pins us with her stare and turns back to face the front.

"You're going to get your gear off for some lady porn merchandise?" I smother my laugh with my hand.

He shakes his head. "*No*... but you are."

My laughter disappears in a flash.

"Like *hell* I am."

"But you owe me, *remember*?" he taunts me.

Oh no fucking way.

I gape at him. "Just say *no* to the guy, I don't see why I have to take your place."

"I owe him."

"So you owe him, and I owe you, so somehow now *I'm* being roped into taking my clothes off?" I demand.

"He needs a sexy teacher or some shit." He runs his hand through his hair. "I don't know, bro, but you're better looking than I am anyway, so you're the man for the job."

"I'm not doing it." I cross my arms firmly across my chest.

"I already gave him your cell number... and told him you would."

I glare at him, and he at least has the good sense to look sheepish about it, although still totally amused.

"I'm going to *kill* you."

"Just pretend it's Perry and one of your private photo-shoots." He sniggers.

Oh no fucking way. I knew letting Perry photograph me in my underwear was a bad idea – no matter how good she insisted I looked.

"Tell me you *didn't* look at my laptop?"

"You shouldn't leave it lying around, man, you never know who might see something they weren't prepared to see."

He's lucky he's broken this to me now, where I can't knock his head in, with hundreds of students and their families watching, and surrounded by every lecturer in the university.

"You better sleep with one eye open, Linc, I've always been good at pay back."

He chuckles. "As long as you show up to that calendar shoot, I don't care about the rest."

"I'm going to kill you. Literally, you're a dead man. I'd say it's been nice knowing you, but it would be a lie."

He chuckles again. "Just think, it could have been worse... you could have been nude."

I groan, and when I glance back at Perry, she's watching the two of us with an amused expression on her face.

Jesus. The things I do for that girl.

OTHER TITLES

Love like Yours Series
Rushed – Book 1
Pierced – Book 2
Hunted – Book 3
Chased – Book 4

Rock Games Novels
Paper, Scissors, Rock: Vol. 1
Hide and Seek: Vol. 2

My Heart Duet
My Heart Needs
My Heart Wants

Calendar Boys Novels
Mr. January
Mr. February
Mr. March
Mr. April
Mr. May
Mr. June
Mr. July
Mr. August

ACKNOWLEDGEMENTS

The songs that inspired this book, *For You I Will* – Teddy Geiger and *Never Seen Anything "Quite Like You"* (Acoustic) – The Script, and *There You Are* -ZAYN.

Thanks so much for reading, I hope you loved Liam and Perry and their off limits relationship as much as I do. They were such fun to write!

Big thanks to my editors, BETA readers and street team, and all the girls in my reader group who have supported me through each release.

Thanks again and I hope you're excited for September!

ABOUT THE AUTHOR

NICOLE S. GOODIN is a romance author and mother of two from Taranaki in the North Island of New Zealand.

In mid-2015, she started to write about a group of characters who wouldn't get out of her head. Her first book, Rushed, was published in mid-2016.

Nicole enjoys long walks on the beach, pillow fights and braiding her friends' hair. She dislikes clichés, talking about herself in the third person, and people who don't understand her sense of humour.

Please feel free to contact her either via her website, email, Instagram, Twitter or on her Facebook page, she would love to hear your feedback. If you're feeling really game, you can even sign up for her newsletter.

Visit www.nicolegoodinauthor.com for more information.

UPCOMING TITLES

Calendar Boys Novels

Mr. September
Mr. October
Mr. November
Mr. December

www.ingramcontent.com/pod-product-compliance
Lightning Source LLC
Chambersburg PA
CBHW021019120726
47905CB00009B/3085